As they walked into the heavily air-conditioned interior of Scooper Duper's, Jessica quickly checked her reflection in the glass door. One of the hair balls had unraveled somewhat and was hanging down the right side of her face like a lifeless snake. Great. How was she supposed to feel charming with limp hair?

"Hey, Jeremy?" She playfully twirled the strand around her finger. "I'm going to the rest room. Would you mind ordering for me?"

"No problem," Jeremy answered, surveying the menu. "What's your poison?"

"Let's see. A double scoop of chocolate-chip cookie dough with little sprinkles of . . . *Will.*"

Jessica's heart stopped. It couldn't be happening. But it was. Standing right in front of her at the cash register was the unmistakable back view of Will Simmons. She recognized the broad shoulders, the left-fingers-in-front-pocket slouch, the boyish waves of sandy hair looping over the back of his baseball cap.

No! Why now? Just when I decided to let it go and have fun.

Don't miss any of the books in SWEET VALLEY HIGH
SENIOR YEAR, an exciting new series from Bantam Books!

Visit the Official Sweet Valley Web Site on the Internet at:

http://www.sweetvalley.com

Francine Pascal's **SVH** senioryear

Boy
Meets
Girl

CREATED BY
FRANCINE PASCAL

BANTAM BOOKS
NEW YORK · TORONTO · LONDON · SYDNEY · AUCKLAND

RL 6, age 12 and up

BOY MEETS GIRL
A Bantam Book / August 1999

Sweet Valley High® is a registered trademark of Francine Pascal.
Conceived by Francine Pascal.
Cover photography by Michael Segal.

Produced by 17th Street Productions,
a division of Daniel Weiss Associates, Inc.
33 West 17th Street
New York, NY 10011.

ISBN: 0-553-48613-6

Published simultaneously in the United States and Canada

Bantam Books are published by Bantam Books, a division of Random
House, Inc. Its trademark, consisting of the words "Bantam Books" and
the portrayal of a rooster, is Registered in U.S. Patent and Trademark
Office and in other countries. Marca Registrada. Bantam Books, 1540
Broadway, New York, New York 10036.

PRINTED IN THE UNITED STATES OF AMERICA

OPM   0 9 8 7 6 5 4 3 2

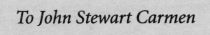

To John Stewart Carmen

Jessica Wakefield

Everything is completely wacked right now.

Melissa is in the hospital. Will is devastated. Elizabeth is fooling around with the guy she's living with who her best friend is totally in love with. And she stole . . . well . . . <u>borrowed</u> his car the other night. That really threw me. It should have given me a little clue that things were about to take an insane turn.

But all I can think about is Jeremy. When he kissed me, nothing else seemed to matter. And everything has mattered <u>so</u> much for so long. . . .

It just makes me want to kiss him again. Really badly.

Elizabeth Wakefield

I never want to kiss Conner McDermott again.

Really. I'm serious.

It's not worth it. It's not worth the look on Maria's face when she caught us. That devastated, pierced, dying-inside look.

Just because I can still feel his soft lips on my neck and his tongue tickling my earlobe and his hands . . . his hands . . .

Okay. So I lied.

I want to kiss him again. But that doesn't mean I will.

Right?

Maria Slater

To: KenQB@swiftnet.com
From: mslater@swiftnet.com
Time: 11:21 A.M.
Subject: <u>Aaaaaaahhh!!!!</u>

Ken—

I know I already left you a message on your machine, and I swear I'm not stalking you. I just saw Conner and Elizabeth kissing. No. Not kissing. <u>Mauling</u> each other right in the pantry in his kitchen. I feel like I'm going to throw up. I swear. And Liz saw me, and she just stood there. She just looked right at me. And then I bolted. Wuss that I am.

She lied to me in the car the other day. She <u>lied!</u> Right to my face.

Should I have tried to talk to her?

Ken. What do I do? What am I going to do?

<u>Call</u> <u>me!!!</u>

Maria

P.S. Sorry I'm a psycho.

Ken Matthews

To: mslater@swiftnet.com
From: KenQB@swiftnet.com
Time: 1:22 P.M.
Subject: <u>Aaaaaaahhh!!!!</u>—Reply

Maria—

I would call, but I'm at my aunt's house and I don't have your number here. Tried information, but you're not listed.

Man, I'm sorry.

To answer your question, I don't think you should have talked to her. You were too upset. And I think it's her turn to come to you now. Then maybe you can talk. Just my opinion.

I hope you're okay. I'll be home tonight and I'll call.

Ken

P.S. You're not a psycho.

CHAPTER 1
Condition Stable

Jeremy Aames picked up his cordless phone, punched two numbers, and then replaced it on the base.

"You can do this," he said to himself. "Just ask her."

After giving countless locker-room pep talks as captain of the Big Mesa football team, Jeremy had learned the value of a personal go-get-'em speech. It was a great way to combat fear and almost always worked. *Almost* always.

"Go for it, Aames," he continued. "You've done it before. This is no different."

Actually . . . it is different, Jeremy reminded himself. *This is Jessica.*

Jessica Wakefield. He saw her dancing sapphire eyes, her playful, slightly pouty mouth, her smooth, golden tan skin—all framed by silky golden hair.

Jeremy was in love. If he wasn't in love, he figured he should probably see a shrink fast. Ever since he and Jessica had shared their first kiss earlier that afternoon, Jeremy hadn't been able to think of anything else. For once even his overly stressful home life had been back-burnered.

1

He leaned against the Formica kitchen counter, head in hands, and sighed. The next logical step, he knew, was to ask her out and establish the traditional dating pattern that real couples shared. Easy, right? Only it wasn't that easy. Jessica deserved better than the stereotypical dinner-and-movie routine—something memorable. Unfortunately Jeremy couldn't afford something memorable. He couldn't even afford something semiforgettable.

Jeremy ran his hand through his dark, spiky bangs, mentally listing all the entertainment possibilities in the valley. The beach? No. Too overdone. Ernie's Bowling Alley? Not exactly the classy setting he was hoping for. The Riot? Too loud and hot. Besides, it wasn't really his scene.

Suddenly an idea came to him. He jumped out of the chair, picked up the phone, and quickly dialed a set of numbers.

"Hello?"

"Hey, Keith. What's up?" Jeremy said brightly.

"What do you want, Jeremy?" Keith asked, already suspicious.

Jeremy knew this wouldn't be easy. Keith Moxon was a friend, but he wasn't the type of person who gave just for the joy of giving. "You still working at the Majestic Theater?" Jeremy asked, picking up a pen and tapping it against the counter.

"Yeah," Keith answered, drawing out his response.

"I was wondering if I could scam a couple of

tickets for tomorrow night's performance," Jeremy said. He quit tapping and started doodling on the front page of the newspaper.

"Hot date?" Keith asked with a chuckle. "You want to take advantage of our dark balcony seats, right?"

"No, Keith." Jeremy's voice went flat. "That's *your* idea of a hot date. I'm more interested in atmosphere."

"Whatever you say." Keith laughed. "The Majestic has plenty of . . . atmosphere."

Jeremy ignored Keith's patronizing tone and looked down at the newspaper. He'd been unconsciously drawing hearts. Jeremy dropped the pen. "What's playing there anyway?" he asked.

"*Romeo and Juliet,* the Bard's star-crossed lovers," Keith announced with appropriate dramatic flair.

"Cool. That's romantic."

"Sure. I guess. If you think gang warfare, murder, and suicide are romantic," Keith joked.

"Whatever," Jeremy said. "So what's this going to cost me?"

"Hmmm. Well, it *is* last minute . . . ," Keith began gleefully.

"Come on, Keith," Jeremy said, rolling his eyes.

"And I *am* risking my reputation for this," Keith continued. "I mean, for all I know, you and your lady friend could end up heckling the actors or disturbing the rest of the audience with loud, wet kissy noises."

Jeremy's patience was rapidly depleting. "You know, *you're* the one who should be onstage—"

"How about your autographed Steve Young card?" Keith interrupted.

"Are you *kidding* me?"

"How special did you say this girl was?"

Jeremy could just imagine Keith's self-satisfied grin. "Fine, fine. Take it," Jeremy grumbled.

"Then there's the little matter of waxing my car . . . ," Keith said.

"No! No way," Jeremy said, slicing his hand through the air as if Keith could see it. "Don't even—"

"Whoa, Aames. Chill," Keith cut in. "I was just kidding. Who *is* this girl you want to impress anyway? Cameron Diaz?"

Jeremy's temper was inching toward the red zone. "Uh-uh. I'm not giving you any information. Just reserve two of your best seats in my name for tomorrow night's show, okay?"

"Sure thing, dude. But don't forget to bring Steve," Keith teased.

Jeremy hung up with a frustrated groan. He couldn't believe he was giving up Steve Young. But then he thought of Jessica, and immediately his mood began to lighten. He'd hand over the *real* Steve Young for a chance with her.

"You can do it, Aames," he mumbled as he carefully punched in her number. His heart was hammering in his ears. "You're in way too deep to blow it now."

"Hello?"

Jeremy immediately recognized Jessica's voice, and a fluttering sensation filled his chest. *Now what?* he wondered, panicking.

"Hey, Jess. It's . . . um . . . it's Jeremy."

"Jeremy!" she exclaimed. "How are you? How's your dad?"

"I'm okay," Jeremy responded. "And my dad's better, but they decided to keep him over one more night to monitor him. He's coming home first thing tomorrow morning."

"That's good to hear," Jessica responded quietly, distractedly.

"Are you okay?" Jeremy asked, his brow creasing.

"Yeah. I'm just . . . dealing with some stress," she said.

Jeremy nodded. "I know about stress. Actually, I own that word. I think you owe me royalties for using it in a sentence."

Jessica laughed, and Jeremy took a deep breath. Time to take the plunge.

"Listen, Jess," he began. "I—I wanted to know if you had any plans for tomorrow night." Jeremy's heart moshed inside him. He gripped the phone with both hands as if an invisible defensive line were rushing after it.

"Well, I'm working until six-thirty, but after that

I'm free. Why?" A playful tone returned to Jessica's voice.

"I was wondering if you'd like to . . . go out." Jeremy let the words tumble free.

"Sounds great! Where to?"

Jeremy's heart jumped. "I . . . um . . ." An idea suddenly took shape in his mind. "I can't tell you. It's a surprise."

"A surprise?" Jessica's pitch rose excitedly. "I left you three hours ago. How did you come up with a surprise date that fast?"

"It's a special talent," Jeremy said, smiling.

"Can I have one hint?" Jessica asked.

"Well . . . it's bigger than a bread box."

"Gee, thanks," she said sarcastically. "At least give me a clue to location."

"It's definitely on this planet. In California, to be more precise." Jeremy leaned back in his chair.

"Okay. I guess that rules out flying the Concorde to Paris."

"Actually, I *will* be transporting you in space and time. But that's the only hint you'll be getting from me," Jeremy said with a grin.

Jessica exhaled loudly. "You realize, of course, that I'm going to get no sleep at all tonight. Thank you very much."

"You're welcome," Jeremy said. He wasn't going to give an inch.

"Well . . . okay," she said. "I'll see you tomorrow."

"See you then," Jeremy said.

They said their good-byes and hung up. Jeremy felt like flying. The secrecy thing had been a stroke of genius. Jessica was definitely intrigued.

Now all he had to do was live up to his own hype.

Will Simmons paced up and down the hospital corridor, inhaling the pungent aroma of alcohol and Pine Sol. Occasionally he would stop and stare fearfully at room 314, as if the heavy oak door were glaring back at him, then slowly resume his restless tour of the hallway.

Why can't I just go in? he wondered. *Why am I so damn scared?*

He knew Melissa was in there, waiting for him. But he wasn't sure how he would react to seeing her. And Melissa would definitely be watching *him* closely, divining all sorts of meaning from his gestures, his expressions, his words.

Will halted once again and looked down at the large floral bouquet he was carrying. His hands gripping the blue glass vase were as white as the roses inside it.

An eerie déjà vu came over him as he thought about all the times he'd stood outside Melissa's house with flowers for her—dates, proms, anniversaries, apologies. Now here he was again, nervously shuffling his feet outside her door. Only this time she was in a hospital gown instead of a to-die-for dress, and her father wasn't going to open the door and greet him with one of his bone-crunching hand-shakes.

White roses were appropriate, right? he wondered nervously. Red was too sexy. Pink was too cheerful. And he was pretty sure everyone sent yellow roses to funerals. White seemed the only acceptable choice at the florist. It was bland, neutral, empty—just the way he felt. But when it had come time to sign the tiny card that came with them, he'd been stumped for hours.

What do you say to a girl who tried to kill herself after you broke up with her?

"It's all right. You can go on in." A nurse in a pink smock top suddenly appeared next to him. She smiled warmly and nodded toward the door. "Go ahead. She's resting comfortably now."

"Thanks," Will replied, trying to hide the exasperation in his voice. No sense dawdling any longer. He took a deep breath of cool, sterile air and pushed into the room.

There she was. Will was relieved to see that Melissa's eyes were closed in a deep sleep. He almost didn't recognize her. Her skin looked drained, and her lips were raw and chapped. Probably, he imagined, from all the tubes they had used to pump the sleeping pills from her stomach.

"Liss?" he whispered.

No response. Will set down the flowers on a

nearby table and ventured closer to the bed. He leaned forward and ran his hand over her hair, which was spread out over the pillow in a mesh of knots and tangles.

"Liss?" he said, even more softly.

He didn't really want to wake her. At least this way he didn't have to worry about saying the wrong thing or giving himself away with his actions. Besides, he told himself, she needed to rest.

Will sat down in a plastic chair and tried to think about what had happened, but his mind kept kicking it back out again. It was just too heavy, too complicated.

Things had been so out of control for so long, he couldn't remember what normal felt like. He and Melissa had always had their dark secrets, but lately all sorts of new craziness had been thrown into the mix. The earthquake. His inability to resist Jessica Wakefield. Melissa freaking out and launching her anti-Jessica smear campaign. Their breakup.

And now this.

Again he tried to let the thoughts in so he could sort through it all, but a rush of anger suddenly came over him, and his brain rejected it. Maybe it was too soon to deal with it. After all, first he had to face Melissa. Then maybe he could face what she had done.

Will stood and took one last, long stare at the pale shell of a person on the hospital bed. Funny.

He'd forgotten how small she was. Melissa had always given the illusion of being someone bigger, stronger—except when she *needed* to be frail.

He leaned over and quickly kissed her forehead. "Bye, Liss," he murmured, then quickly turned and left the room.

Good-bye was the only word he had for her.

Elizabeth Wakefield stood staring into her dresser mirror, contemplating the soap opera her life had become. An autobiography of the first few weeks of school would contain more twists and turns than Highway 1's ocean stretch.

Was it just that very morning Maria had caught Elizabeth and Conner kissing? Elizabeth felt worn, like she'd been reliving the moment for weeks. The tears streaming down Maria's face. Running after her best friend but having absolutely nothing to say in her own defense. She knew she should call Maria to apologize and see if she was all right. But how in the world could Elizabeth explain her actions to Maria when she couldn't understand them herself?

For as long as she could remember, Elizabeth had been branded with such adjectives as *sensible, practical, responsible,* and *polite.* She felt a pang of regret as she mentally recited the words and watched her eyes cloud over. She was no longer any of those things. She'd moved away from her family, blown off countless *Oracle* staff meetings, and spent most of her time hanging out at clubs or panting over Conner McDermott. Who *was* this person staring back at her?

She leaned closer and inspected her features. For some reason, she expected to find wrinkles.

"Hey."

Elizabeth jumped as Conner's face appeared next to her reflection, his forehead creased and his green eyes almost concerned.

Elizabeth turned around to face him, and Conner shoved his hands into the back pockets of his well-worn jeans. "So . . . this Maria thing is a major mess."

Leave it to Conner to sum things up so blithely. "Major," Elizabeth agreed, feeling as if there were a brick wall between them. She looked at the floor, wishing that Conner would reach out and hold her —tell her everything was going to be okay. But he wasn't exactly the emotional type. She was surprised he'd even stopped by her room.

"Elizabeth," he began, lifting his arms. She felt an exhilarating rush of anticipation as she prepared to cuddle into them, but he simply set his hands on top of her shoulders. "Listen," he said, "I have an idea."

"What?" she asked, looking into his eyes. A determined expression had fixed his chiseled features. *So he does have a solution,* she thought warmly. He actually did care.

"I'm going to back off a bit and let you sort things out."

11

Elizabeth felt her stomach tighten. "You're going to . . . back off?" she repeated.

"Yeah," he replied. Then, as if to illustrate his determination, he took his hands from her shoulders and crossed them over his chest, stepping back. "I know you need some time right now to work things out with Maria, and it'll be better if I'm not in the way."

"Not in the way?" she echoed.

Conflicting emotions swirled inside her. On the one hand, Conner was making perfect sense. It would be easier to fix things with Maria if she and Conner put whatever it was they had going on hold for a while. But she *really* didn't want to. It had taken them so long just to get to this standing-here-awkwardly-and-occasionally-kissing phase. She couldn't drop it now.

"It's not like it's forever," Conner said. "No big deal, really."

His pitch was all wrong—almost eager. Did he *want* to back off?

No, she thought, pushing aside her fear. *He's only thinking of me and what's best for everyone. This can't be easy for him . . . right?*

She took a deep breath. "Okay. You're right. Just give me some time to explain things to Maria and let her get used to the situation." It wrenched her insides to utter the words, but she managed a brave smile.

Conner's mouth curled up in a look of—what

12

was it? Affection? Relief? Resignation? As usual Elizabeth couldn't quite pin it down. Then, before she could even react, Conner leaned forward and caught her lips in a sweet, eager, penetrating kiss. He placed his hands on the sides of her face, cupping her cheekbones as Elizabeth fought to control her frantically fluttering heart.

When he broke away, he looked her directly in the eye. "It won't be forever," he repeated. Elizabeth could only manage a slight nod.

Conner turned to go, and Elizabeth sat down shakily on the edge of the bed. "Thanks for understanding," she said, her voice oddly clear.

"Yeah," he said with a slight shrug. "I'll leave you alone." He held her with the same indecipherable gaze for a few seconds. Then he turned and left, shutting the door behind him.

Elizabeth felt the room grow cold and empty. She fought the urge to follow Conner and tell him to forget the whole thing. That the last thing he should do was back off. But that wasn't an option. Right now Maria was most important. Besides, the sooner she smoothed things out with her, the sooner she and Conner could really be together.

Maria Slater sat up against the headboard of her queen-size sleigh bed and stared at the mosaic of university catalogs and pamphlets scattered across her quilt.

So it was back to her egghead existence. *Might as well look to the future,* she thought. As far as she was concerned, there was nothing left at high school worth getting excited about.

She reached for a Princeton course schedule and began flipping through it, forcing herself to push aside all thoughts of the day's events and focus instead on the fine-print entries. *Sex Roles in Modern Society? That sounds cool. Interpersonal Communication? Hmmm. Maybe. Molecular Biology?*

Her index finger passed over dozens of potential courses—dozens of ways to drown her mind with facts.

Let's see . . . Self-Paced Astronomy? Art History? Music Appreciation?

Music . . .

Immediately thoughts of Conner flashed through Maria's mind, as if someone were working a cruel yet eerily authentic View-Master inside her. Conner playing guitar. Conner staring at her with one of his dangerously sexy expressions. Conner with Elizabeth, their faces mashed together in a passionate kiss.

Maria could feel her stomach knotting up. *Okay. Scratch music class.*

Suddenly the phone on the nightstand rang, startling her. She just stared at it. After this morning's drama, screening calls seemed the best way to go.

Maria heard the series of clicks and loud beeps of the ancient answering machine. Then Elizabeth Wakefield's voice filled her bedroom.

14

"Hi. Maria? It's Elizabeth. Are you there? I really need to speak with you. Maria? Please pick up."

A dense heaviness pressed against Maria's chest. Somewhere under the layers of pain her conscience told her to pick up the phone. But she couldn't. Instead she sat frozen against her mahogany headboard, desperately trying to concentrate on Stanford University's journalism-degree plan.

Forget Ken's e-mailed advice. Maria just didn't want to deal with this. Not yet.

"Are you there, Maria?" There was a short pause, and then Elizabeth's tone grew softer. "Listen, I'm . . . uh . . . I'm real sorry about . . . what happened this morning. God! You must hate me, but I can explain. Really." A long sigh followed.

Maria covered her head with a pillow, wishing her eardrums would spontaneously burst. Why didn't Elizabeth just get a clue and hang up? Maria had thought she'd be safe for a while in her bedroom, barricaded against the rest of the world. But no. Now the nightmare was sneaking in over the telephone lines, forcing her to listen to the ugly reality she was stuck in. And to top it all off, the volume control on the machine was busted. She couldn't even turn it down.

"I never meant for things to get this messed up," Elizabeth's voice continued. "I tried to fight the way I felt about him. I really did. And I promise nothing happened when you guys were together . . . nothing

15

really. I guess I should have told you sooner. I just didn't know how. . . ."

Stop! Maria's brain screamed. *Just shut up and leave me alone!* Part of her wanted to leap off the bed and stomp on the answering machine until it buckled and died, but she didn't move. She couldn't.

Maria had always been this way. Instead of growing hot with rage whenever people hurt her, she simply turned cold—retreating to a quiet place deep within herself. Maria loved to act, but she didn't go for drama in her private life. Unfortunately she'd had a lot of drama thrust upon her lately.

Elizabeth groaned. "This is stupid," she said. "I can't believe I'm blabbing all this to a machine. Anyway . . . *please* call me, Maria. You're my best friend. I know we can figure this out." There was another long, pitiful sigh, followed by the click of the line disconnecting.

Maria let herself breathe again.

She glanced back down at the university schedules lying open in her lap. Maybe she should just forget about college. After all, what could it teach her about life that she hadn't already learned?

Will Simmons

~~Get well soon,~~

~~Hope you're feeling better.~~

~~Why did you have to go and do a thing like this?~~

~~I want you safe, but I don't want you back. I love you, but I don't love you anymore. I hate you for doing this, but I don't hate you. . . .~~

Thinking of you.
~~Love,~~
~~Yours,~~
~~Best wishes,~~
—Will

Senior Poll Category #2:
Most Likely to Win an Academy
Award (Best Actor/Actress)

Please <u>make</u> <u>only</u> <u>one</u> <u>nomination</u>.

<u>Elizabeth Wakefield</u>
Maria Slater (Jessica "I'm-ready-for-my-close-up" Wakefield would kill me if she saw this.)

<u>Maria Slater</u>
Elizabeth Wakefield— Who knew she was such a fake?

<u>TIA RAMIREZ</u>
MARIA SLATER

<u>Andy Marsden</u>
Tia Ramirez—Backyard theater queen of the world. She was Annie. I was (and I'm not proud of this) Sandy. The dog.

Conner McDermott
Tia Ramirez—She once made me play
Daddy Warbucks to her Annie.

Will Simmons
No clue

Ken Matthews
Maria Slater

Melissa Fox
Tia Ramirez—I was Pepper,
one of Annie's orphan friends.
We were, like, eight years old.

Jessica Wakefield
Maria Slater —— I can have humility.

CHAPTER
All Apologies
2

As soon as she parked the Jeep and approached the school on Monday morning, Jessica could tell things were different. Instead of the lazy, procrastinated pace typical of students returning after a fun-filled weekend, everyone stood buzzing about in neat little clusters all over the school's front lawn.

Even before the first high-pitched whispers reached her ears, Jessica knew the topic of everyone's conversation. Obviously news of Melissa's suicide attempt had already made the rounds.

As she headed down the front sidewalk, Jessica could pick up fragments of different conversations like a slowly turning radio dial.

"I heard it was Valium."

"No, Xanax."

"Did she leave a note?"

"First she didn't make cheerleading captain. Then Will . . ."

Will! Jessica felt her throat constrict. She remembered the haggard look on Will's face at Melissa's house yesterday and wondered if he would show up at school. What must he be going through?

In the lobby Jessica was immediately confronted by a wall of noise. She tried desperately to shut down the auditory center of her brain.

"Jess!" Enid Rollins walked up, her eyes as big as compact discs. "Did you hear about Melissa?"

"Um . . . yeah," Jessica replied, continuing toward the lockers. Enid fell into step beside her.

"God! Who would have thought things were so bad?" Enid went on, throwing her arms out at her sides. "I mean, she seemed to have everything, don't you think? She's beautiful, she's popular . . . she's got an awesome boyfriend."

Jessica didn't answer. She debated whether it would be wise to swerve left and accidentally slam Enid into a row of lockers, knocking her senseless.

"At least she's going to be okay." Enid accelerated her step to match Jessica's. "I heard Gina Cho tell Tarlise McRaney that Melissa's out of danger. Apparently she can even go home in a few days."

Jessica stopped suddenly. "She's going to be okay," she repeated. *Thank God!*

"That's right," Enid replied, interpreting Jessica's statement as a question. "They said she'll probably come back to school before the end of the month. Apparently they feel the routine will be good for her so that things can go back to the way they used to be."

"Right . . ." Jessica nodded distractedly. "Look, I've got to get some things ready for class."

Jessica hastily veered down an adjoining corridor and wove around gossip clusters, afraid to look back in case Enid decided to descend on her with more juicy details. Finally she reached her locker and quickly opened it, feeling somewhat sheltered behind the tiny barricade of the gray-green slotted door. Only then did she allow her thoughts to take shape.

So Melissa was going to be all right. For that, Jessica was thankful. But was everything really going to go back to the way it used to be?

For weeks Jessica had been praying that something else would come along and replace her as Most Gossiped About. And now it had happened. As awful as it was, a small, selfish part of her was relieved.

Maria stood onstage with one hand pressed to her ear and the other pushing buttons on an invisible console.

"Lieutenant Uhura," Aaron Dallas said, swiveling around on the center bench. "Put a channel through to the Klingon vessel."

"Aye, aye, sir," she replied, busily pantomiming his command. "Channel patched through."

Aaron stood up and assumed a heroic pose, his blond hair shining under the stage lights. "This is Captain Kirk of the U.S.S. *Enterprise* speaking to the Klingon command," he shouted into the air. "Let it be known that we will continue firing upon your ship, taking hostages, and calling you silly names unless you beam over twenty cases of blood wine and three of your hottest women. . . ."

"Freeze!"

Renee Talbot walked onstage and tapped Mr. Spock's shoulder, taking his place.

Oh, no, Maria thought from her paralyzed stance, *not* her! *She always makes us act out—*

"What are we going to do, Jack?" Renee began, restarting the scene. "The water is freezing, and a life jacket will wrinkle my dress."

All that Titanic *schmaltz.*

Maria groaned as inaudibly as she could, jumped off her bench, and splashed "overboard." Why did students always see playing Freeze as a chance to act out their Hollywood fantasies? Normally Maria loved drama class, but this exercise always made her feel ridiculous.

She treaded the icy water of the Atlantic, crying out for a lifeboat, a Starbucks cappuccino, a new director. Meanwhile Aaron chased Renee around the stage, begging to draw her picture as she changed into her swimwear. The audience laughed halfheartedly, but unfortunately no one called "freeze." Maria prayed they'd take her place next.

Maybe she should have stayed home today. She could be lounging around in bed, eating Ben & Jerry's and watching the Cartoon Network. But no. Good ol' responsible Maria. Couldn't blow her attendance record. Besides, she figured coming to school would keep her busy and would help take her mind off Conner and Elizabeth. Of course, it also meant she'd have to somehow avoid seeing them all day.

"I'm king of the world!" Aaron was shouting from atop the downstage bench. "I can get ten million per picture, and I don't even shave yet!"

This is getting old, Maria thought as she lay back and pretended to do the backstroke.

Actually, it was a fitting analogy. Just when she thought her life was cruising along perfectly, *bam,* an iceberg bearing an uncanny resemblance to her best friend jolted her from her happy existence. Now she was simply treading water.

If only someone would trade places with her in real life . . .

"All right! We're done for the day!" Ms. Delaney called. "Good job, everyone."

Maria stood and hopped off the stage in a flash. She grabbed her bag and started for the back of the auditorium before Tia or Jessica or anyone else remotely associated with Elizabeth could talk to her.

"Don't forget about auditions for the fall play!" Ms. Delaney called after the class. "The sign-up sheet is by the door, and I want to see all of you there."

"Maria! Are you going to try out?"

Maria stiffened but adopted a casual expression as she turned to face Tia. The girl was actually

24

skipping up the aisle, pen in hand, her thick brown hair swinging around her shoulders.

"I don't think so," Maria answered. Actually, she *knew* she wasn't going to try out for the play. Everyone always got so cutthroat about it, and she hated the catty way people handled callbacks and the eventual cast posting. Maria preferred not to get involved.

"I don't think I'm going to do it either," Jessica said, joining them. Maria's stomach turned just from looking at Elizabeth's twin.

"Why not?" Tia asked.

"Oh, I really want to put myself in the spotlight in front of all the people who hate me," Jessica said almost lightheartedly. "As if I don't get enough abuse during the day."

"Whatever," Tia said, rolling her eyes. She turned and grinned at Maria. For some reason, even Tia's smile was scraping at Maria's nerves. She backed up an inch. "If Jessica isn't going to do it, you *have* to. Someone has to keep me company," Tia said.

"Well, it's not going to be me," Maria said, with a bit more bite than she intended. Tia's face fell, and Jessica looked at the thin, brown carpeting. At that moment the bell rang. Maria pushed through the thick wooden door and let it slam behind her. She hated when she heard herself throwing off bitchy comments, but being around those two had pretty much pushed her over the edge. Tia was Conner's best friend, and Jessica was Elizabeth's sister. They had to know what was going on with Conner and Elizabeth. They'd probably been laughing at her behind her back for days.

Just one more reason to hate Elizabeth.

Well, it's official, Elizabeth thought as she hoisted her book bag onto her shoulder and joined the rushing current of students in the corridor. *Conner is definitely avoiding me.*

He'd joined Quigley's class late, flashed her a vague smile, made no further eye contact, and then immediately left the room when the bell rang. She knew he was only giving her space to work things out with Maria and that she'd agreed to it, but she hadn't expected him to back off so *completely.*

At least it's only for a little while, she thought. *And it's for a good cause.*

Elizabeth sighed heavily. Somehow she just couldn't fully convince herself that being away from Conner was the greatest idea. If she couldn't handle the new distance between them for one class period, how could she endure it for a week? Or two?

Maybe she could put a positive spin on this. Ever since things had heated up between them, she hadn't really been certain how to act around Conner. What do you say to a guy at the breakfast table when just hours before you were kissing him so passionately, you thought you might spontaneously combust?

And at night, when the day's distractions were over, all that separated them from each other was a thin plaster wall. Elizabeth knew things could get real heavy, real fast, if they weren't cautious. *Real* heavy.

Elizabeth was used to relationships developing along a predictable, fairly slow course. But she and Conner had gone from ice cold to searing heat in just a flash, making Elizabeth feel both giddy and jet-lagged.

Were they even a couple?

No . . . she couldn't even think about that until she faced Maria and apologized.

Elizabeth suddenly felt a massive weight anchor her down—and it wasn't her book bag. The look on Maria's face when she had caught Elizabeth and Conner kissing was deeply etched into Elizabeth's mind. The girl had been crushed, flattened . . . obliterated. Elizabeth knew firsthand how painful it was to see Conner with someone else. And now she was inflicting that pain herself.

There had to be some way she could fix things with Maria. Some flogging ritual she could undertake to prove how sorry she was. Elizabeth turned and detoured down another hallway. She spotted Maria right away, standing at her locker, talking to Ken Matthews.

They seemed almost cozy. Something about the way they were turned toward each other and the small amount of space between them . . .

Nah, Elizabeth thought, shaking her head. *They're probably just talking about their history class.* Those two had less than nothing in common.

"Maria!" Elizabeth called.

Ken and Maria stopped talking and looked at her. Elizabeth couldn't be sure, but she thought she saw them exchange a brief yet meaningful glance. For a split second she feared Maria might have told Ken everything but then quickly pushed the thought aside. *You're paranoid,* she scolded herself. *Maria barely knows Ken.* She took a deep breath and approached them.

"Hi, Ken," she said quickly. "What's up?"

"Hi, Elizabeth," he replied. He was smiling, but his eyes looked sad. She knew that sadness—the pain of losing Olivia—and she wondered if it would ever leave his eyes.

A new feeling of despair tugged at her heart, but she made herself ignore it. *Don't think about the past,* she told herself. *Focus on the here and now.* She casually wedged a shoulder between them and turned toward Maria.

"Hey, um, Maria? Could we talk for a sec?" She was surprised by how small and squeaky her voice sounded.

"Uh . . . I've got to get to class," Ken said, straightening up and backing down the hallway a step. "Talk to you later, Maria. Bye, Elizabeth."

"Bye," Elizabeth called after him. She watched as

Maria flashed him a helpless stare. When Ken turned and began heading down the corridor, Maria barely brushed her eyes over Elizabeth before tearing open her locker and loudly rifling through its contents.

"I'm running late," Maria said coolly.

"Maria, just let me explain," Elizabeth pleaded, deciding not to point out that Maria didn't seem at all rushed as she stood talking to Ken. "I'm so, so sorry. For everything. I've been a complete idiot," Elizabeth said, moving her face into Maria's line of vision as she rummaged through her books.

Elizabeth paused, waiting for some sort of response—a spoken reply, an expression, a whack upside the head with a physics textbook—anything. But Maria continued digging through her locker as if Elizabeth wasn't even there.

"Look, I . . . I never meant for anything to happen between me and Conner—it just did. I never, ever, *ever* meant to hurt you."

Again Elizabeth cringed. Too many *evers* made it sound insincere. Speech was just too insufficient to convey her feelings. If only she could lay a hand on Maria's forehead and transmit her thoughts, make her see everything she'd gone through lately. If only she hadn't waited until now to tell her.

"Maria, I just don't know what to say," Elizabeth continued. Her first perfect statement of their conversation. "I'm just *so* sorry."

"Forget about it," Maria said suddenly. "It's in the past."

Elizabeth's heart leaped. Maria was saying exactly what she wanted to hear, but her voice was too loud and quick to come across as believable. And she still avoided looking Elizabeth in the eye.

Elizabeth took a deep breath. "About Conner—"

"You can have him," Maria said, fumbling with her bag. "None of that matters anymore. I'm through with Conner."

Then, as if to punctuate her statement, she shut her locker with a fierce *bang* and sped off down the hallway, leaving Elizabeth drowning in the sound waves.

Elizabeth grasped her books against her chest as fear gripped her by the throat. Maria might have said she was through with Conner, but Elizabeth had a sinking feeling that her best friend was actually through with her.

Will Simmons

If I hear one more person tell me they're sorry, I'm going to scream. I will literally run into the street, shouting the worst obscenities I can think of.

All I've heard today from the kids, the teachers, even guys on the team is that they are all "so sorry to hear about what happened to Melissa."

They're not sorry. The whole situation is sorry. _I'm_ sorry. In fact, I'm probably the sorriest jerk in the universe.

Sorry doesn't get anyone anywhere.

Ken Matthews

Why are people always so thrilled to hear horrible news? Does hearing about other people's misfortune feed some sort of twisted, morbid hunger inside us? Are we humans or overgrown vultures in trendy clothes?

All anyone can talk about today is Melissa Fox. Their eyes spark up and their voices get eager as if it's all one big, exciting show just for them. It makes me sick.

This isn't entertainment. It's real life— and death. I should know. When I see the tired, detached look on Will Simmons's face, it makes me remember losing Olivia and how no one knew how to act around me afterward.

When you're in the middle of a nightmare, you need everything around you to be normal— for people to behave the way they've always behaved. Instead everyone freaks. They either avoid you or want you to drag all the pain you're feeling inside out into the open. There's no escape.

Things will never, ever be the same for Will. But at least Melissa survived. That means he can survive too.

CHAPTER
Strike One
3

Jeremy lay sprawled on the living-room floor, surveying the Dining Out section of the newspaper. Over the stereo some singer was asking where people were going without knowing the way.

"You got me," Jeremy mumbled back to the band. "I have no idea myself."

When Jeremy had returned home from school, he'd found his father sleeping peacefully in his parents' room. Jeremy had prepared the pull-out couch in the living room for his dad, but Mr. Aames had said he'd be more comfortable in his own bed.

Seeing him there made it seem as if nothing had changed, except his bedside table was now lined with translucent orange pharmacy bottles. Heart medication. Blood-pressure medication. Stress relievers. Whatever they were, the sight of them had made Jeremy ill. His mother had taken the day off to get his father settled, and she'd run out for groceries with his two little sisters. Jeremy figured he had about an hour of peace and quiet before mayhem resumed.

He wanted to find just the right place to take Jessica to dinner before the play. Unfortunately he couldn't afford a restaurant with tuxedoed maitre d's and valet parking. In fact, his budget was closer to the drive-through-window range. But Jessica deserved better than that.

"Hey, son." Jeremy was startled to see his father looming in the doorway in his slippers and bathrobe.

"Dad! What are you doing up? You're supposed to be resting." He quickly stood and ran to the stereo cabinet. "I'm sorry. Was the music too loud?"

"No, no. It's fine." Mr. Aames waved his hand at Jeremy and shuffled into the room. "Why aren't you at football practice?"

"There wasn't one today. It's a Monday after a win," Jeremy answered, turning off the CD player.

"Oh." His father's brow furrowed. "I guess it is Monday. Well, they all run together for me now."

Jeremy studied his father's pale face. His brown eyes still looked dull and watery, and his cheeks were sunken and drawn. "Really, Dad. Shouldn't you be lying down?"

Mr. Aames sighed and shook his head. "I've spent so much time staring at the ceiling in that room, I'm starting to see pictures in the paint strokes. It won't hurt me to be vertical for a while." He pointed to the open newspaper. "What's with the restaurant ads?"

"I've got a date tonight, but nothing seems right," Jeremy said glumly.

"A date?" Mr. Aames said. "Don't you have to work at that coffee place?"

"House of Java," Jeremy said with a nod. "Ally gave me a few days off. I know I need the money, but the pressure was starting to get to me, and I—"

Jeremy saw his father's brow furrow with concern and almost bit his tongue. His father was stressed enough. He didn't need to hear Jeremy whining.

"Anyway," Jeremy said. "Now I have time for a date."

"Well, I'm glad to hear it," Mr. Aames said. "Why don't you just pick any old place? It's not the food; it's the company that counts," Mr. Aames said as he settled onto the couch.

"But this is our first date," Jeremy said, staring desperately at the ads. "It's gotta be good."

"Oh?" Mr. Aames raised his eyebrows at Jeremy. "This girl is pretty special, huh?"

Jeremy shrugged indifferently, but he could feel his face ripen, giving him away.

"Have you thought about a picnic?" his father asked.

"You mean . . . you want *me* to cook?"

"Sure. Why not?" his dad replied slowly. "The weather's great. Flowers are still in bloom. What could be more romantic than sitting on a quilt in some nice outdoor setting?"

"I don't know, Dad," Jeremy said doubtfully. There *was* a park next to the Majestic Theater. It had a grassy yard that sloped down to a big duck pond full of reeds and water lilies. It might be okay for an intimate picnic. "What would I make?" Jeremy asked. "I don't think my tuna sandwiches will cut it."

"No, no. Not tuna." Mr. Aames smiled, slowly rose from the couch, and headed into the hallway. "Come with me." He beckoned.

Mr. Aames shuffled into the kitchen and began rummaging through cupboards, boxes, and pantry shelves. Jeremy followed, marveling at his dad's new-found enthusiasm. He hadn't seen him this energetic in weeks, and the guy had just been released from the hospital.

"Let's see. . . . We've got noodles, onions, some canned broth. . . ." His dad's voice grew muffled as he stuck his head in the refrigerator. "This girl eat meat?"

"Yeah," Jeremy replied. "Yeah, I think so."

"Good. I believe we have all the fixings for a stir-fry."

Jeremy watched as his dad began piling mush-rooms, garlic, frozen broccoli, rice, and a plastic-wrapped raw chicken breast on the nearby counter. "Uh, Dad. You know, you don't have to do this," he said, wondering if his father should be expending so much energy. His breathing was starting to sound la-bored.

His father ignored the comment. "How much time do you have?"

"She's supposed to meet me at seven," Jeremy

replied, glancing at his watch. He had a few hours.

"Excellent." Mr. Aames nodded approvingly. "That'll be just right. I'm thinking we can pack up some stir-fry chicken and vegetables over rice, a bottle of sparkling water, and maybe even throw in some of Emma and Trisha's homemade cookies for dessert. How does that sound?"

Jeremy was speechless. He couldn't remember the last time he had seen that eager glint in his father's eyes. Or the last time they'd tackled a project together. "Great, Dad," he said eventually, swallowing back the emotion in his throat. "That sounds great."

Jessica raced the Jeep up the Fowlers' driveway, hopped out, and glanced at her watch. Only fourteen minutes after six. She'd had to fake severe stomach pains in order to get off half an hour early from work, but at least now she had plenty of time to shower and change before meeting Jeremy.

Throughout her shift at House of Java—when she wasn't doubling over with possible appendicitis pangs—she fantasized about the big, secretive date Jeremy had planned.

She remembered he once told her that his dad had taken private flying lessons. Could he be planning to fly her someplace exotic on a private jet? Hmmm. Seemed unlikely for a school night. Besides, she knew he and his family couldn't afford those things anymore.

Tia had once told everyone about this special anniversary date her boyfriend, Angel, worked out that was all a big scavenger hunt. She would drive to a special spot where she'd get a gift and a large pink envelope directing her to the next stop. There she would find another gift and another envelope, and so on until she finally met him at a private dining room, where he was waiting with flowers, dinner, and hired musicians. That sort of thing was more Jeremy's style but probably a bit much for a first date.

What were they going to do? The possibilities were making Jessica nervous. On the one hand, she liked surprises. They kept you on your toes. But on the other hand, it was good to be prepared. After all, what if she dressed totally wrong for the evening? Or spent forever on a hairstyle only to have it messed up by some wild ride on a rented Harley-Davidson?

Whatever he had in store for her, she was sure it would be wonderful. Just the thought of being with Jeremy for a night out gave her a cozy feeling inside, like slowly sipping a cup of cocoa.

Jessica skipped up the front steps and entered the house, almost colliding with her mother in the foyer.

"Oh, Jessica. You're home," Mrs. Wakefield said, trying to place a hand on her daughter's bouncing frame. "Jeremy just called."

"Really?" Jessica stopped short. "What did he say?"

"He said you should meet him at seven o'clock at 2007 Isabelle Avenue."

Ah, the adventure begins, Jessica thought, revving up again. "Was that it?"

"Yes. That was all," Mrs. Wakefield said with a smile.

"Thanks, Mom," Jessica said, racing up the stairs.

Isabelle Avenue. 2007 Isabelle Avenue, she chanted all the way through her shower. It was her only clue so far. The address itself meant nothing, but it seemed to hold wonderful promise.

The matter of wardrobe posed some potential risks. Let's see. . . . If she dressed too casually, she might risk embarrassing herself or making it appear as if she didn't care much. Better to be overdressed than underdressed.

Of course, then there was the problem of shoes. There could be lots of walking involved or slippery marble staircases. But some places didn't allow tennis shoes—even the glittery platform kind.

She must have missed this article in *Cosmopolitan,* "How to Dress for a Big Surprise Date." Men obviously never thought about such consequences.

After trying on half the contents of her closet, Jessica finally settled on her favorite black dress. It was the one thing that always seemed appropriate, no matter what the occasion. And it never let her down. She slipped on her black suede sling backs and pearl-drop earrings to complete the ensemble.

"All set," she said, staring at her reflection in the mirror. Her eyes were wide and glittering with anticipation. It had been a long time since she felt this psyched about anything.

Minutes later she was driving down Central, singing with the radio at full volume to quell her nerves. By the time she turned onto Isabelle Avenue, her hands were almost too sweaty to maintain a grip on the steering wheel. Jessica squinted at the addresses, her excitement doubling with every mile. She passed the dry cleaners at 2001 Isabelle Avenue, the movie-rental place at 2003, and the hair salon at 2005. Finally at 2007 she pulled into the parking lot of . . . Fantasy Island Fun House?

"A kiddie arcade?" Jessica said aloud.

Jessica eased the Jeep into a space and remained frozen in her seat. She waited for Jeremy to come running up to her window, laughing and singing out, "Just kidding!" She checked the area for any large pink envelopes directing her to another location. She even looked up in case a private jet were circling above. But there was nothing. Just a group of glassy-eyed kids blinking at the setting sun as they emerged from the building.

Oh, well. Guess this is the place, she thought, hopping out of the car.

Okay, so this wasn't exactly what she had in mind, and it was a little tame for her flirty dress. But it was cute, potentially. And she definitely had to give him points for originality.

*   *   *

Okay, so she was a half hour late. Thirty-five minutes, to be exact. No reason to freak out, right?

Jeremy walked down the length of the sidewalk and checked the parking lot for the fourteenth time. Jessica and her Jeep were nowhere in sight.

By now some of the cast members were showing up at the theater, many already in full makeup and costume. A few of them cut through the park and noticed Jeremy, sitting forlornly on the quilt next to a picnic basket and bottle of sparkling water, and gave him strange looks. Jeremy thought it was ironic that guys in tights and eyeliner would find him odd, but he did feel like a pretty pathetic dork.

He checked his watch again. Thirty-eight minutes past the hour.

No need to panic. There were plenty of reasonable explanations. She could have gotten held up at work or stuck in traffic or struck by lightning or . . .

Or decided she'd rather not go out with you after all?

"No," he said aloud. Something was wrong. Jessica would never stand him up.

He left the blanket and wandered into the playhouse lobby, locating a pay phone. Jessica's mom picked up on the first ring.

"Hello, Mrs. Wakefield? This is Jeremy. I . . . um . . . I've been waiting here for half an hour now, and Jessica still hasn't shown up. I was just getting worried, you know, that something might have happened to her?" His stomach was doing somersaults.

41

"Jeremy! I'm so glad you called!" Mrs. Wakefield exclaimed. The high timbre of her voice made Jeremy brace for bad news. "Jessica just phoned. She said she's been waiting a long time and wanted me to repeat the address you left. I told her 2007 Isabelle Avenue, just like you said, but that's where she's been all along. Where are *you?*"

"I'm at the Majestic Theater, at 2007 Isabelle *Court*," he explained, breathing a sigh of relief.

Mrs. Wakefield gasped audibly. "Oh, Jeremy! I'm so sorry! I must have switched the two streets. She ended up at Fantasy Island Fun House instead."

"Don't worry about it," Jeremy said with a laugh. "I'll just drive over there and pick her up. No problem."

After reassuring Mrs. Wakefield that her mistake was completely understandable, Jeremy loaded up the picnic things and drove to the opposite side of town. *Fantasy Island Fun House?* he thought, shaking his head. *What sort of weird date must Jessica think I had planned?*

As he pulled into the arcade parking lot, he spotted Jessica immediately. She was sitting next to a statue of a giant carousel horse, looking weary, bored, and absolutely beautiful. Her face brightened up when she saw him.

"Jeremy! I was so worried! Where have you been?" She stood up and smiled as he approached.

"Verona, Italy," he quipped.

"Ookay," she said, her eyebrows knitting together.

"Your mom got the addresses mixed up," Jeremy explained. "I was at the Majestic Theater. We were going to see *Romeo and Juliet.*"

Jessica's eyes gleamed. "Oh, can we still go?"

Jeremy glanced down at his watch and shook his head. "They'll be dead by the time we get there."

"Oh, well," Jessica said with a laugh. "We kind of knew the ending anyway." She paused and frowned down at the sidewalk. "I'm sorry about the mix-up. You went to all that trouble for nothing."

"It's okay," Jeremy said, trying to sound unaffected. Actually, he *was* disappointed that his carefully planned night had tanked, but it wasn't Jessica's fault. At least they were together now. "I packed a picnic dinner. As long as we're here, why don't we eat it inside, then maybe play some Foosball?"

"Okay," she said with a shrug. "But I have to say, I feel a little overdressed."

Jeremy smiled. "Who cares? Maybe those video nerds will tear their eyes away from the screens for once."

Elizabeth stood at the bottom of the Sandborns' staircase, staring up at the unfriendly darkness. There was no sound at all—except for the residual ringing in her ears from the loud music at the Riot.

She had just returned from hanging out with Tia, Angel, and Andy all evening. Conner hadn't been

43

home when they picked her up, so she had written him a quick note telling him where they'd be. He never showed. Still, she ended up having a great time—or at least half of her did. The other half had kept constant watch on the door.

Slowly, purposefully, Elizabeth climbed the stairs. Staying at the Sandborns' house over the last few weeks, Elizabeth had learned which steps were the creakiest and usually avoided them. This night she deliberately set her weight on them.

A little play of what would follow was already composed in her mind—complete with stage directions and cheesy background music. As she reached the second-story landing, Conner would open his bedroom door. Their eyes would meet. Not a word would be spoken. They'd simply fall into each other's arms and kiss as if no one else existed in the world.

Or so she hoped.

Forget her conscience. She *so* wanted to see him. But she didn't want him to *know* she wanted to see him. She wanted him to be wanting her, but she didn't know how to *tell* if he was wanting her. He said he was giving her space to work things out, but she didn't know if that meant avoiding her entirely or only in public places. Unfortunately, short of a sudden gift of telepathy, there was no way for her to know for certain.

There was a precise term for her situation. Elizabeth had looked it up in the dictionary earlier.

She liked the word. The *con* part reminded her of Conner's name. The *un* provided a prefix to everything she was feeling—unbalanced, unarmed, uncertain. And the *drum* part seemed to symbolize the staccato beat her heart pounded out whenever she was with him.

Finally Elizabeth reached the top step and paused, waiting. Conner's door remained shut, but the thin rectangle of light beneath it toyed with her. Conner was in there, awake. Possibly even thinking of her. Possibly waiting for her.

Let's see. . . . What would be a good reason to disturb him? She heard a noise? She was going for a snack and thought he might be hungry? She suddenly and tragically lost her sight and wandered into his room by mistake? Or maybe . . . maybe she missed him and ached to feel his lips on hers before turning in?

"Hello, Elizabeth."

Elizabeth sucked in her breath and quickly spun around to see Mrs. Sandborn standing in the hallway outside her bedroom.

"H-hello," Elizabeth replied, trying to appear casual. "I'm sorry. Did I wake you up?"

"Oh, no. I wasn't sleeping." Mrs. Sandborn smiled and gestured at her outfit, a long, floral skirt and neatly pressed white blouse. Elizabeth was surprised to see her dressed up so nicely.

"Of course," Elizabeth mumbled sheepishly. "It's kind of dark. I, um, couldn't see you very well."

"That's all right." Mrs. Sandborn laughed lightly. "Did you have a nice evening?"

"Yes. Thank you," Elizabeth replied. She hadn't had such a lengthy conversation with Conner's mother in weeks. Usually Mrs. Sandborn was napping or wandering around looking half asleep. A mumbled "hello" was her typical greeting—if even that much. Elizabeth had always assumed Mrs. Sandborn was either ill or depressed but never asked about it. It wasn't her place.

But tonight she seemed so . . . cool and coherent. Maybe she had finally snapped out of her funk—whatever it had been.

"Well, it is late. I really should turn in," Mrs. Sandborn said, opening her bedroom door. "Good night, Elizabeth."

"Good night."

As soon as Mrs. Sandborn shut her door, Elizabeth turned back toward Conner's room. He must have overheard that conversation. Would he come out and say good night?

As if in response, the light under Conner's door suddenly flickered out. Elizabeth sighed in defeat, walked into her room, and flopped back onto her bed.

None of this would be so hard if she were certain of Conner's feelings. But even after all the stolen moments they had shared, she had no idea how he felt about her. His total elusiveness was part of what made him Conner. And Elizabeth knew it was part of what made her want him so much.

But it didn't make her life any less frustrating.

"Die, *T. rex!* Die!" Jessica squealed, aiming her plastic laser gun at the all-too-lifelike dinosaur coming right at her and Jeremy. She pumped her trigger finger wildly.

"This is insane," Jeremy said, holding up his gun with both arms. "My muscles are actually going to be sore from this."

Jessica screeched as she took one last shot and the *T. rex* finally reared its head and fell over. Jeremy grinned and watched her laugh triumphantly. Who knew a girl that beautiful would enjoy playing video games among a bunch of spaced-out kids?

"Would you believe I'm sweating?" Jessica said, shaking out her hand.

"I know," Jeremy said as he flexed his fingers. "I think it's time for a soothing game of old-fashioned pinball."

Suddenly a siren went off inside the building, and the under-seventeen population of the arcade groaned in unison. "Fantasy Island will be closing in fifteen minutes!" a voice announced over the loudspeaker.

Jeremy's mood sank. "Maybe we should call it a night," he said.

Jessica reached out and grabbed his wrist, turning it to check his watch. "I can't believe it's practically ten," she said.

"Time flies, I guess," Jeremy said. He looked around the kid-infested room, feeling morose. Although the evening had been fun, it hadn't lived up to his grand expectations. Jessica climbed out of the booth that housed the dinosaur game and held back the curtain as Jeremy followed.

"You know," he said as they headed for the door, "there's a new comedy club downtown, and I hear they have a great show on Tuesday nights. What do you say we check it out?"

"I'm supposed to work tomorrow night, but . . ." She met his eyes and smiled slyly. "Sure. I'll think of something convincing. After all, I *am* taking theater class. I'll tell Ally that my heart is heavy with recent misfortune and alas! I shall not be able to adequately perform my services for the evening," Jessica said, delivering the last part in a perfect English accent.

Jeremy held out his arm and said in what he hoped was a passable accent, "Dear lady, if it please you, I shall accompany you to your steed. Where, pray tell, is he parked?"

"Anon," she replied, laughing as she pointed across the parking lot.

Outside, the dark lavender light from the fluorescent lamps blurred edges and boundaries, making the outline of her hand against his soft and indistinct—as if they'd been melded together. When they reached her car, Jessica turned and smiled at him. She looked so beautiful. Jeremy felt as light and buoyant as one of the helium-filled balloons they sold inside. He knew he had to kiss her. Her eyes sparkled, and her mouth parted slightly. That was all the invitation he needed. Catching his breath, he leaned toward her, tilting his head at a perfect angle to bring his lips to hers.

Suddenly, just before contact, a high-pitched scream cut through the evening air. Jeremy jumped backward.

"*No!* I don't want to go home! No! No! No!"

The noise emanated from an ice-cream-stained eight-year-old who was being led out to a nearby minivan by his mother. "Playtime is over," she kept saying. "Time to go to bed."

"No! I don't want to! I want to play Sonic! Please! I don't want to go home!"

Jessica and Jeremy watched as the mother patiently wiped his face, disarmed him of a plastic pirate dagger, and buckled him into the backseat. Once the van had driven off, Jeremy turned back toward Jessica, and they both laughed awkwardly.

"I sort of know how that little guy feels," Jeremy said. "I don't want to go home either." He stared into Jessica's blue-green eyes, wanting to try again to kiss her, but the momentum was gone.

Jessica grinned. "Playtime is over. But we *do* have tomorrow." She hopped into the Jeep and rolled down the window. "I really had a good time," she said, revving the engine.

"Me too," Jeremy answered, smiling.

He stood there alone, watching until her car drove out of sight.

Conner McDermott

Things are going well. And that worries me.
I've learned to be suspicious when things go right.
Usually it's just the calm before the storm. If you
start thinking that your problems are gone and
from now on everything will be sunshine and happy
faces, you'll drop your guard. That's when life sneaks
up behind you and shoves you in the dirt.

That's why I'm avoiding Elizabeth. I can't let
myself get any closer to her. I've already been stupid
enough to develop . . . feelings . . . for her. And any
further involvement is just asking for a major wipeout.

When Maria figured things out between me and
Elizabeth and booked, I could tell it was the first
sign of trouble. I realized if I didn't do something
fast, everything would start going bust. So I told
Elizabeth we needed to back off for a while. It

was the mature thing to do. That way no one gets hurt.

And now I have the perfect excuse to stay away from her and not screw things up. And maybe, just maybe, if I avoid things for a while, I can prolong this quiet, almost happy state my life is in at the moment. Because it won't last. Sooner or later, things will get messed up with Elizabeth. That's a no-brainer.

Besides, I have to be on the alert anyway. Mom's been doing fine for a while now, which is good. But lately she's been hanging out at the country club again, which is <u>always</u>, always bad.

Storm clouds are definitely on the horizon. Now is not the time to get soft.

Jessica Wakefield

Tuesday, 8:42 A.M.

[In a small, weak voice]

Hello, Ally? It's Jessica. I'm just calling to let you know that I won't be able to make it in today. . . . I'm so sorry, but I still have that weird stomach-virus thing . . . Yeah, the doctor says it's going around right now and that it's highly contagious. Can't be around people or food. And being around coffee products could interfere with the medicine I'm taking. . . . Anyway, I hope my canceling doesn't really put you in a bind or anything. . . . Uh, yeah, I suppose you could ask Jeremy to fill in for me . . . if he doesn't have other plans. . . .

CHAPTER
Battle of Wills
4

Sitting on the gym's hardwood floor after school on Tuesday, Jessica touched her forehead to her knee, feeling a slight tug in her tendon. She repeated the same move on her other leg, then spread her legs wide and touched her head to the floor. Soon she could feel her muscles grow warm and pliant, relaxing her whole body. After a pop quiz in history, a lunch of paper-thin, paper-tasting pizza, and listening to people's speculations about Melissa's mental state for the second day in a row, Jessica needed a moment of peace.

She sat up straight and closed her eyes, breathing slowly and deeply. Suddenly something hard and hollow sounding smacked the back of her head.

"Ow!" she cried, whirling around.

Cherie Reese and Gina Cho stood next to her, fierce hatred cemented on their faces. Cherie held a megaphone in her hands—the obvious instrument of attack.

"Oh," Cherie said in her empty voice. "Did I accidentally hit something, Gina?"

54

"Yeah. Something vile. Better go shower it off," Gina said, raising a perfectly plucked eyebrow.

Jessica could feel herself instantly refilling with tension. Normally she would ignore Gina and Cherie and wait for them to go away or get up and leave the room. But something inside Jessica suddenly snapped, and she scrambled to her feet.

"You did that on purpose," she said. "I don't care what you guys think of me, but everything should be neutral during practice."

Gina blinked in obvious surprise before finding her voice. "Well, you've got some nerve showing your face at practice after what you did."

"Yeah. You should be at church, begging forgiveness," Cherie added, tossing her curly red hair over her shoulder.

Here we go again, Jessica thought. She could feel the familiar churning in her stomach. *What made me think the abuse was finally over? They'll never stop.*

Cherie took a step toward Jessica, her nose and cheeks flaming to match her hair. Jessica had seen a variety of disdainful expressions on Cherie's face over the past few weeks, but this was by far the worst. "Because of you, Melissa's in a hospital right now," she spat. "She almost died, and it's all your fault."

"What?" Jessica exclaimed almost noiselessly. "You're blaming me for . . ." It was too horrible to say. She had thought they were starting in with the usual line of trash about her, but now she realized it was worse than that. *Much* worse. They actually thought she was responsible for what happened to Melissa?

By now the rest of the cheerleaders had abandoned their exercises and stood watching the heated exchange from a safe distance. Jessica hoped Lila and Amy wouldn't jump into the fray to make it four against one.

"All right." Tia stepped out of the group and moved in between Jessica and the others, holding up her hands. "All of you need to chill out and get back to warm-ups. Coach will be in here soon."

Jessica just stood there, numb. Cherie and Gina lifted their chins victoriously and started to turn away.

"Killer," Gina muttered under her breath.

Jessica felt as if that one word had pierced her, puncturing her insides, and a sudden uncontrollable fury came rushing out.

"*Stop!*" Jessica seethed through clenched teeth. Gina, Cherie, and the rest of the gym's occupants gaped at her. "I have had *enough* of you two talking dirt and acting like you're so high-and-mighty! *You're* the ones who've been totally out of line!"

Tia placed a hand on Jessica's arm. "Jess, this isn't the place—"

"No! Let me finish!" Jessica wrenched away from Tia and stalked toward Cherie and Gina until only inches separated them. She could see their eyes grow

56

wide, but they stood their ground. "I'm not taking this abuse anymore! For weeks you've done nothing but torment me, and I haven't done a thing to deserve it."

Cherie snorted. "Right. Like you didn't blab to everyone about trying to steal Will from Melissa."

"I never knew they were a couple!" Jessica hollered. It was the defense she'd been trying to use throughout her entire ordeal. She would have put it on a T-shirt if she thought it would help. But everyone seemed far too happy to think of her as the evil seductress. "Will could have told me about Melissa, but he didn't, did he? Have you ever stopped to consider that?"

Gina and Cherie exchanged a brief, indecipherable glance. Then Gina placed her hand on her hip. "Well, now that Melissa's out of the picture for a while, I'm sure you'll take advantage of the situation," she said.

"What?" Jessica could feel her wrath intensify. "Are you insane? If you two want to attack someone for what happened to Melissa, you should talk to Will—not me!"

Cherie fixed Jessica with a glacial stare. "Will loves Melissa. The sooner you get that through your head, the better."

"Yeah," Gina jumped in. *"You're* the one who tried to mess up their lives. All we're doing is trying to protect our friend."

"Oh, really?" Jessica asked. "Well, maybe if you guys acted more like her friends instead of mindless followers, you would have realized she was miserable enough to try to kill herself. Maybe you could have been there to stop her."

Cherie sucked in her breath as the color drained from her cheeks. Gina's eyes narrowed, and she lifted her chin defiantly, but Jessica could tell she'd struck where it hurt the most. She felt a twinge of guilt for her accusations, but her anger was overwhelming. Weeks of pent-up emotions were spewing forth, and there was nothing she could do to stop them. She didn't *want* to stop them.

"How can you accuse me of being this horrible person when you don't even know me? I've never done anything to you, but you've spent all your free time making my life a living hell. And you call *me* evil," Jessica continued ranting. "You've lied and cheated and mocked me to everyone. And what good has it done? Huh? Has it helped Melissa? Has it helped you?"

By now Gina and Cherie were completely speechless—two glaring, twitching lumps. But Jessica still wasn't finished. She inched even closer and let go one final blow, using the last of her pent-up rage as fuel.

"If you guys want to go on fooling yourself about who's right here and who's wrong, be my guest," Jessica said. "But from now on . . . stay away from me! And stay out of my life!"

58

The words reverberated off the gymnasium walls for a fraction of a second, and then everything was quiet. Jessica kept her eyes fixed on Cherie and Gina, who each looked a size or two smaller. The rest of the cheerleaders glanced nervously at one another, too shocked to speak. Jessica couldn't be sure, but out of the corner of her eye she thought she perceived a slight smile on Lila Fowler's face.

Suddenly Jessica felt strangely weak. Her hands trembled, and her knees felt as if they could give way any second.

Thankfully, right at that moment Coach Laufeld pushed through the wooden gym doors. "All right, girls, get into places. Wakefield! Why are you just standing there? Let's move!"

"Coach?" Jessica whispered, crossing the room somewhat unsteadily. "Could I please be excused to the rest room?"

"Go ahead," Coach replied. "But don't take long."

Jessica raced down the hallway, a feeling of triumph fluttering in her chest. It had felt so good to finally get back at Cherie and Gina. She felt purged, cleansed. She felt strong.

But by the time she made it to the seclusion of an empty bathroom stall, her sense of victory started to fade. Jessica slumped down onto the tile floor as new, unsettling thoughts seeped slowly into the hole where her pain and anger had been.

What if Gina and Cherie were right? she wondered

anxiously. *What if I really did have something to do with Melissa's suicide attempt?*

No. It wasn't possible. Jessica had to push away the thought and focus on something else. She pulled herself off the floor and took a deep breath.

"Focus on . . . Jeremy," she told herself. "Think about the incredible time you're going to have tonight."

But instead of Jeremy's warm brown eyes, an image of Will's pale, shell-shocked expression flashed into her mind and icy fear skittered down her spine. *What about Will?* she thought. *Does he blame me too?*

"Aames, can you come in here for a second?" Coach Anderson stood like a sentry in the doorway to his office, watching as the football players marched past on their way to the practice field.

What now? Jeremy thought as he broke out of the tide of football players and ambled into the tiny, glass-walled office at the corner of the locker room. The coach motioned to a small, wooden chair opposite his desk, where Jeremy plunked himself down.

Jeremy figured Coach Anderson was about to ream him out. Lately at football practices Jeremy had been running on autopilot, sometimes making key mistakes. He was overdue for the old "you're-not-giving-110-percent" talk.

Coach Anderson plopped into the vinyl swivel

chair behind his desk and exhaled audibly. Jeremy stared into his huge meatball of a face, waiting for the attack.

"Aames, I just want you to know," the lecture began, "that I heard about your father."

Jeremy sighed. "Oh," he said. *Who could have told him?* A couple of his buddies on the team knew about his dad. He supposed one of them might have said something.

"Yep, I, uh . . . I know, it must be . . . ," Coach stammered, nodding vigorously as if he made perfect sense. Jeremy had never seen him look so cramped and uncomfortable. Suddenly he wished Coach were yelling at him instead. "What I'm trying to say is that I'm sorry," Coach finally managed. "I know it's hard."

"Thanks," Jeremy replied. He had no idea what else to say. For the next full minute they simply nodded at each other and shifted uneasily in their seats.

"You see, my brother had a heart attack not too long ago," Coach continued. "It was real tough for everyone. He was so weak. The whole family had to rearrange their schedules to stay with him constantly. I even took several sick days of my own just to go be by his side, shooting the breeze or reading *Sports Illustrated* to him." He paused, bobbing his head up and down again. "But in the end, it paid off. He's completely recovered."

"That's great," Jeremy exclaimed, squirming even

61

more restlessly. He knew the coach was just trying to connect with him, show him he understood. But Jeremy couldn't help thinking about his dad lying in bed all day, completely alone. What was it his father had said yesterday? That he was going nuts looking at the ceiling? An invisible fist squeezed Jeremy's heart. Maybe he *should* be doing more.

But Dad's getting better, he told himself. *Besides, what can I do? Quit my job? Quit school? Quit football—the one thing Dad is most proud of?*

"Yep. It takes teamwork and commitment," Coach continued, pushing his blue baseball cap back on his head. "But it is possible to get through a tough battle like this one and come out ahead. You got me?"

"Right," Jeremy replied, wishing he could suddenly dematerialize and reappear hundreds of miles away. He was never very good with the face-off-across-a-desk form of talking. And when the topic was his own private life, it took on a new displeasure. He felt like he was being held down in the chair by invisible straps.

"Well, anyhow"—Coach rose from his seat to signal the end of the conversation—"if there's anything I can do, you just let me know." He smiled at Jeremy, looking very pleased with himself.

"Thanks," Jeremy replied, standing. "Thanks a lot, Coach."

"No problem. Now go out there and knock heads."

Jeremy walked out of the office as fast as he could. Back in the locker room he leaned against the wall and exhaled slowly. An image of his dad, weak and alone in his bed, kept swirling through his mind. He briefly considered getting a copy of the latest *Sports Illustrated* and racing to his father's side, but he knew he couldn't miss another practice. Besides, what about tomorrow and the day after that?

If only he could clone himself. One Jeremy could go home and sit with his dad, another could finish his homework, and another could run pass patterns until he bonded spiritually with the football.

A nice piece of science fiction, but he couldn't think about that now. First he had to make it through practice. Then he had a date with the most beautiful creature on earth.

His worries would still be there tomorrow.

Elizabeth walked into the *Oracle* office, trying on a facial expression she hoped was neither too cheerful nor too somber. Sure enough, Maria was there, stapling the sports and club schedules onto the newspaper bulletin board.

"Maria," Elizabeth said breathlessly. It sounded more like a reply to an unheard question than a greeting. "Hey."

"Hi," Maria replied, continuing with her stapling. Her voice wasn't exactly angry, but it wasn't friendly either. Instead it was just empty—void of any tonal quality that could clue Elizabeth in on underlying emotions.

"I, um . . . I've been looking for you all day," Elizabeth remarked. "I was hoping we could, maybe, go for coffee and talk?"

"No," came Maria's hollow reply. She picked up another rectangular sheet of paper and positioned it neatly on the cork board. *Bam! Bam!* Elizabeth winced as the stapler shot forth its metal hooks, skewering the paper and cork grain.

"Please, Maria?" She ventured closer, nervously squeezing one of her hands in the other.

"I don't think so," Maria replied. As she turned and fetched another schedule off the table, Maria's eyes passed over the floor tiles, the tables, the fluorescents—but not Elizabeth. Elizabeth had the uneasy feeling that she had suddenly become transparent.

"You're my best friend, Maria. Why won't you just talk to me?" Elizabeth asked. So much for her self-control. Now she sounded like a whiny six-year-old.

Finally Maria turned and faced her. "There's nothing more to say," she declared calmly.

At least she's making eye contact, Elizabeth thought. But it still wasn't enough. She wanted Maria to scream at her, burst into tears, bounce the stapler off her head—anything to purge this awkwardness between them.

"Look, just one cup of coffee," Elizabeth attempted

again. "You don't have to say anything. *I'll* do all the talking. Please? It can't hurt."

A look of pain flashed over Maria's features and then was gone. "I said no, Liz," she mumbled, then quickly turned back to the bulletin board. *Bam! Bam!* Elizabeth jumped slightly. Could Maria be envisioning her face up there?

Okay. At least there had been a brief glimmer of emotion, and she did call Elizabeth by name. Elizabeth was grasping at any hopeful shreds she could find, as if she'd broken something valuable and needed to retrieve the pieces in order to fix it.

"Okay, then," Elizabeth began. "We can talk here, while you work. I know you're totally furious with me, and I don't blame you. I just want to explain that—"

Maria closed her eyes and tensed up her shoulders. "Look, I'll make this easy for you. You want my blessing to go after Conner? Fine. You have it. Don't waste time feeling guilty or trying to justify things to me—just go for it." She fixed Elizabeth with a stony expression. "But don't expect our friendship to continue."

Elizabeth shivered, and hot tears sprang to her eyes. She knew Maria was angry, furious even. But she couldn't be giving up on their friendship after all they'd been through together. For years Maria had held Elizabeth's secrets, bolstered her confidence, supported her through family skirmishes, breakups, and bad hairstyles. And now, because of one mistake—an awful mistake, of course—Maria was going to simply walk away?

She might as well have pushed Elizabeth against the display board and nailed her up with thousands of razor-sharp staples. Maybe even stabbed a note to her chest detailing Elizabeth's horrible sins for the rest of the world to read. It would have hurt less.

"You can't mean that," Elizabeth said shakily. "I'm sorry for what I did. You've got to believe me."

Maria turned back around and began stapling a paper she'd already affixed to the board. *Bam!* "That's all I'm going to say, Elizabeth." *Bam!* "Why don't you get out of here?" *Bam!* "I'm sure Conner's waiting for you."

Jessica Wakefield and Tia Ramirez

AUDITION PRACTICE. CAFETERIA. TAKE ONE.

Tia: What are you trying to tell me?

Jessica: I'm trying to tell you that your son is dead. I'm sorry, madam.

Tia: [*Huge gasp*] There must be *some* kind of mistake.

Jessica: Wait a minute. Time-out. Tia, what was that?

Tia: [*Miffed*] What was what?

Jessica: *Some* kind of mistake. That's totally the wrong word to emphasize.

Tia: Well, it's *totally* my audition.

Andy: [*Through a mouthful of food*] Well, you're both *totally* annoying.

Jessica: [*Rolls her eyes at Andy*] Let's try it again. [*Clears her throat*] I'm trying to tell you

that your son is dead. I'm
sorry, madam.

Tia: There must be some kind of
mistake!

         [*Jessica laughs*]

Tia: What now?

Jessica: *Days of Our Lives* ask for an
audition tape?

Tia: [*Crosses her arms over her
chest*] Fine, Ms. Streep. How
would you do it?

Jessica: [*Stricken*] There must be some
kind of mistake.

Tia: Blah, blah, bland. Here. How
about this? There *must* be
some kind of *mistake.*

Jessica: Nope.

Tia: *There* must be—

Jessica: Nope.

Tia: *There must* be some kind of—

Andy: There must be some way to
make you shut up.

Jessica: There must be—

Tia: There must *be*—

Jessica: There must be some—

       [*Bell rings*]

Andy: There is a God!

CHAPTER

Strike Two

5

"Liz, I swear my hair is rebelling. It looks like it's been cranked out of a Play-Doh Fun Factory. You think Lila might have put Elmer's glue in my conditioner or something?" Jessica asked.

Elizabeth watched as her sister rummaged through a stack of multicolored barrettes, selected a large banana-shaped clip, and pulled back her hair with it. "Your hair looks fine, Jess," she said, glancing around Jessica's posh room at the Fowlers'.

Jessica turned her face from side to side, studying herself in the dresser mirror. "Now I look like a preschool teacher," she said with a groan. She yanked the clip from her head, taking a few hairs with it, and sighed heavily. "Except for maybe shaving my hair off entirely, I'm out of ideas."

"You ought to wear it up and pull loose strands down around your face," Elizabeth suggested. "That'll look sexy."

Jessica turned around and narrowed her eyes at Elizabeth. "*Excuse* me? Shouldn't you be telling me to blot my lipstick and avoid anything too low cut?"

Elizabeth pretended to look put out, but inwardly she was smiling. She knew she had never been known for her sense of fun. Of course, she had always had close friendships and an ironclad code of ethics as well. Now that those were out the window, the trade-off seemed a little imbalanced.

"Here, let me help." Elizabeth picked up a brush and began running it through Jessica's fine blond mane, eager for something else to focus on. The mechanical motions took her back several years to when she and Jessica used to play with each other's hair, practicing various grown-up-looking styles. Back when things were easy.

"Liz?" Jessica's voice sounded far away, and Elizabeth wondered if she might be remembering the same thing. "Can I ask you something?"

"What is it, Jess?" Elizabeth stared at her sister's downcast image in the dresser mirror.

Jessica closed her eyes and sucked in her breath. "Tell me the truth. Do you think I could be responsible for what happened to Melissa?"

"You're messing with me, right?" Elizabeth set down the brush and turned Jessica toward her. "Is this a trick question?"

Jessica shrugged weakly and stared down at her hands.

"Jess! There's no way you could be responsible for what happened! How could you even think so?"

"I don't know." Jessica gestured helplessly.

71

"Maybe if I hadn't flirted with Will and started up this whole mess, maybe she wouldn't have gone over the edge like that."

Elizabeth grabbed Jessica by her shoulders. "Listen to me. *You've* been the victim throughout this whole deal. Whatever Melissa's problems are, they're much deeper than all this. There's a lot we don't know about her."

"Yeah, I guess you're right," Jessica mumbled, still staring at the carpet.

"Hey. Why are you wasting time thinking about this anyway?" Elizabeth asked, picking up the hairbrush and playfully whacking Jessica on her head. "You have a hot date to get ready for and you're stuck with Play-Doh hair."

"You said it wasn't that bad!" Jessica protested.

Elizabeth laughed. Over the years she had learned it was impossible for anyone to counsel Jessica out of the dumps. But if one could redirect her thoughts to more pleasant subjects (like guys or chocolate or guys or cheerleading or guys), she was usually able to sweep her worries aside.

"Seriously, Jess. You deserve to go out and have an incredible time tonight."

The light behind Jessica's eyes switched to high beam. "You know . . . you're right," she said softly.

"Hey, don't sound so surprised." Elizabeth laughed. "I'm always right."

"Well, I wouldn't go that far," Jessica said with a smirk.

"So what are you going to wear tonight? Maybe that will help you solve your hairstyle dilemma."

"Actually, I'm not sure what to wear. Jeremy's taking me to that new comedy club, and I don't know what the seating is like," Jessica said, picking up a beaded necklace and holding it under her chin.

"Seating? Is that important?" Elizabeth asked.

"Yeah. It's important," Jessica exclaimed, dropping the necklace. "If we're sitting at tables, I need to wear something to play up my upper torso, like a scooped neckline and a delicate strand of beads. If we're on stools, I can emphasize my legs more—maybe wear shimmery hose and strappy shoes. Then there's the whole lighting thing."

"Lighting thing?" Elizabeth repeated, her brows knitting.

"Of course," Jessica said, obviously exasperated. "With lamplight or candles you have to wear glittery makeup and go a little heavier on the colors. But don't ever do that with ultrabright fluorescents or it's like, 'Hello. My name's Elvira. What's yours?'"

Elizabeth shrugged helplessly. Leave it to Jessica to raise dressing for a date to a high art.

She watched in awe and amusement as her sister painstakingly tried on most of what she owned before settling on a wine-colored sheath dress and lacy coverlet. Jessica then studied herself walking in four pairs of shoes before deciding on the gold platforms.

"All set," Jessica said, slowly turning around to show Elizabeth the full effect. Then she faced her reflection and frowned. "Only I still have no clue about my hair. Let's see . . . I need something hip but not too radical. Any ideas?"

"I know!" Elizabeth exclaimed. "You could do those little . . . hair-ball things!"

"Hair balls?" Jessica repeated, wrinkling up her nose. "As in, the stuff cats vomit up?"

"Uh, no. It's cool. Megan showed me how to do this the other night."

She took a thin cord of Jessica's hair from the top of her head and twisted it over and over until it finally wound into a tidy knot. Then she secured it with two hairpins. "Ta da! See? It's sort of a mini–Princess Leia bun."

"I don't know, Elizabeth. It kind of looks like an alien growth or something," Jessica said.

"That's because I've only done one. You need the full effect." Elizabeth picked up another lock of hair and twisted it down, then repeated her styling until she had made a nice, even row across the top of Jessica's head.

"Well, what do you think?" Elizabeth asked when she was finished.

Jessica turned her head back and forth, scowling at her image. "Are you sure I don't look like one of the Teletubbies?"

"No. You look gorgeous—if I do say so myself."

"Oh, well." Jessica sighed, narrowing her eyes. "Maybe I can provide the comics with some great improv material, huh?"

"Whatever," Elizabeth said. "Jeremy's tongue is going to hit the floor when he sees you."

"There's an attractive mental picture," Jessica quipped, putting the finishing touches on her eye shadow.

A bittersweet feeling came over Elizabeth as she watched her twin. As happy as she was for her, she couldn't help but feel envious too. She recognized that eager giddiness one feels in the early stages of dating. She and Conner had bypassed that. They'd never have it.

"Come on." Jessica started steering Elizabeth toward the door. "Jeremy will be here any minute. In fact, he might be downstairs suffering through one of Dad's stories right now. Maybe he and I can drop you off at the Sandborns' on our way to the club?"

"No, that's all right," Elizabeth replied quickly. "Mom can take me later."

"You sure? It's really no problem," Jessica said, tossing makeup into her satin handbag.

Elizabeth nodded, afraid actual speech might trigger a set of tears. The thought of tagging along on Jessica and Jeremy's date, even for a couple of minutes, made her feel even sorrier for herself.

Besides, she was in no hurry to get back to the Sandborn house and all its closed doors.

"I'll be fine, Jess," she lied. "Go on and have an amazing time."

"Okay. Suit yourself," Jessica said, shrugging. She snapped her bag shut and headed out into the hallway.

"And don't let things get too steamed up between you two," Elizabeth called after her. "You might pop your hair loose."

Jeremy reached out to ring the doorbell at the Fowler house and felt his right arm muscles protest. His entire body felt as if it had been through a mulcher.

All through practice he hadn't been able to get Coach's speech out of his mind, and he'd ended up dropping passes, missing blocks, and just basically sucking. If Coach hadn't known about Jeremy's problems at home and been so chummy, he'd have hung him from the goalpost for sure.

Suddenly the door opened and the mental image of Coach Anderson's scowling face was replaced by a live vision of Jessica.

"Hey!" she greeted him.

"Wow," he exclaimed, taking in her hair, her dress, her blazing smile. "You look . . ." *Luscious* was the first word to come to mind, but he decided that might be too graphic for a take-two first date. "You look beautiful."

Her grin gained even higher wattage. "Thanks," she replied. "So do you. Except . . ." She bent closer to inspect his face. "You seem to have some mud on your cheek."

Jeremy reddened and rubbed both sides of his nose. "Sorry. Guess I missed a spot," he mumbled. "Practice was a killer today."

"I hear you," she said. "Mine was a major pain too." She pulled a pink Kleenex out of her shiny handbag, blotted it against her tongue, and gently wiped Jeremy's right cheekbone. The gesture made Jeremy lose his breath.

"There," she exclaimed, pulling back and studying his face. "All gone." She tossed the wad of tissue onto an ornate wooden table and walked back onto the stoop, closing the door behind her. The few seconds gave Jeremy enough time to slow his pulse.

He walked her to his old Mercedes and opened the passenger door for her. By the time he climbed in, the car interior had already filled with the spicy scent of Jessica's perfume. Immediately the memory of their first kiss began rolling in his mind. He glanced over at Jessica, focusing on her full, plum-painted lips.

"What?" Jessica asked. "Is something wrong?"

Jeremy's gaze jumped up to her eyes and furrowed brow. "Uh, no. Nothing's wrong. Let's go."

Get a grip, Aames, he told himself as he backed out of the Fowlers' long, sloping driveway.

Traditionally the kissing comes at the end of the evening. You haven't even left her house yet.

As Jeremy concentrated on driving down the neighborhood's palm-tree-lined boulevard, he absently reached up to rub his stiff neck.

"What happened?" Jessica asked, leaning over slightly to examine him. "Did you hurt yourself at practice?"

"You could say that," Jeremy replied, shrugging. "I was practically playing Twister with a two-hundred-fifty-pound lineman. I think his profile is permanently pressed into my backbone."

"Do they always let the defense maul their star receivers at practice?" Jessica asked.

"It was my fault, actually. I wasn't paying attention." He frowned, remembering how lousy he'd played that afternoon. After missing Saturday's game and messing up continuously during practice, Jeremy was beginning to sense the other players' exasperation.

I'm letting them down, he thought glumly. *The team, my dad, my teachers. I'm letting everyone down.* He could feel that familiar tightness, like a giant wad of liquid cement, returning to the pit of his stomach. All sorts of people were relying on him, and he couldn't do right by any of them—not one.

A soft noise beside him broke Jeremy out of his thoughts. Jessica was saying something.

"I'm sorry," he said. "What was that?"

Jessica smiled wryly. "I said I bet it's hard to focus with everything else going on in your life. How's your dad doing?"

"Fine," he answered, trying to sound solidly convincing. What else could he say? That his father seemed physically better but was probably slowly going crazy with boredom? That he really couldn't comment on his father's health since he always had better things to do than spend time with him?

What if Coach was right about his brother's recovery—that it was all due to his family being there all the time? Did that mean Jeremy's father wouldn't get any better since he was always alone?

He sighed and gripped the steering wheel so tight, his skin seemed to form a molecular bond with the vinyl.

"Hey, um . . . let me know if I can help, okay?" Jessica said softly.

Jeremy exhaled slowly, trying to relax. "Thanks, Jessica," he replied. "So . . . ," he began, searching for another line of conversation that would dispel the awkwardness. "You said your practice was tough too?"

It was Jessica's turn to look strained. "Uh, yeah," she said. "I just had to . . . make up for lost time. I've gone a little soft lately."

He watched as Jessica sighed and leaned her head against the car window, nervously twisting the strap of her purse. He tried to think of another, safer topic, but right at that moment they pulled onto Central Drive and found themselves immersed in bumper-to-bumper traffic.

"Oh, great!" Jeremy exclaimed. Just what he needed.

Jeremy tried to see down the road. As far as he could tell, they'd be keeping a ten-mile-per-hour pace all the way to the next county.

"Are we going to be late?" Jessica asked, sitting up straight again.

He glanced at the clock on the dashboard. It was seven-fifty. The show didn't begin until eight o'clock, but they still had to make it all the way across town.

"I don't know," he mumbled. "I'm sorry, Jess."

Keith had referred to Romeo and Juliet as being star-crossed lovers, and Jeremy was beginning to understand how they must have felt. Why was it that everything he planned for him and Jessica ended up as a big fiasco?

"Hey, that's okay," she said, putting on a game face. "We'll get there eventually. It's just nice to be out, you know?"

"Yeah." They exchanged warm smiles.

The car ahead of them picked up speed, and Jeremy was just about to hit the accelerator when a white convertible suddenly cut in front of him.

Jeremy felt his temper surge. "*Hey!* Use a signal, jerk! What is this? Driving by telepathy?"

Jessica jumped slightly.

"Sorry," he said again. "I, uh, hate it when people do that."

He turned his attention back to the road, cursing himself inwardly. He'd had such big plans for the evening, and now he was just praying they'd arrive at their destination without any major embarrassments. So far their date had about as much forward progress as their drive down the highway. Creep along slowly, then screech to a halt—with no relief in sight. Jeremy could feel the ends of his nerves fraying like worn shoelaces.

Finally, just when Jeremy was beginning to think they'd spend the entire evening staring at the white lines of Central Avenue, the traffic gradually picked up a steady pace. Within a few minutes they were pulling into the parking lot of the Funny Farm. Jeremy breathed a sigh of relief.

"We're only fifteen minutes late," Jeremy remarked. "I'm sure they'll still let us in."

After parking in what could have been another time zone entirely, they hopped out of the car and quickly hurried into the lounge. A curly-haired guy with glasses greeted them inside.

"Excellent! More rabble to feed to the lions. Welcome, strangers." The guy wore an official Funny Farm pair of rainbow-striped overalls, a white T-shirt, and a name tag that read Astro.

"Are we too late for the show?" Jeremy asked. "Can we still go in?"

Astro's large eyes focused on them from behind his bifocals and he grinned broadly, reminding Jeremy of an oversized Muppet. "Not to worry. The good news is that the show only started a couple of minutes ago. You haven't missed much. The bad news is that I first need to check your IDs, take your blood, and perform a routine strip search."

Jeremy and Jessica exchanged uneasy glances.

"Whoops! I'm sorry, that's only for Saturday-night shows!" Astro exclaimed, slapping his palm against his forehead. "But I do need to check your IDs."

"Why is that?" Jeremy asked hesitantly.

"Because we only allow in jaded twenty-one-year-olds and over. Even though our material is NC-17 at the worst, we do serve alcohol, so we can't allow the perky crowd."

This can't be happening! Jeremy's mind screamed. *Not again!* He felt like ripping up the swirl-patterned carpet and tunneling through the floor to escape.

"But what if we promise not to drink?" Jessica asked Astro hopefully.

"Sorry, kiddos." Astro shrugged apologetically. "No can do. The manager would likely chop me up and flush me down the toilet if I break the rule. You understand."

They nodded dejectedly and walked back out to the parking lot.

"I'm sorry, Jessica," Jeremy said, feeling as if the only thing he'd done all evening was apologize.

"Don't worry about it," Jessica said brightly. "You didn't know. So . . . what now?"

Jeremy sighed and glanced around him. Traffic on Central was moving along only slightly faster, and the thought of driving someplace far didn't appeal to him. He finally noticed a pink neon sign in the strip mall down the street—Scooper Duper's Ice Cream Shop.

"You feel like ice cream?" he asked apprehensively.

She followed his gaze and smiled. "Sure! Why not?"

As they walked back to the Mercedes, its engine fan still whirring, Jeremy could only shake his head in disbelief.

First the kiddie arcade and now ice cream, he thought glumly. Where were they going to end up next? The playground jungle gym?

Jessica leaned her head against the headrest and sighed. Why couldn't she just relax? Okay, so the evening's plans went bust and Jeremy had been kind of edgy, but she certainly wasn't helping matters any.

If only she could stop thinking about Melissa.

Her mind was at war with itself—two sides arguing Melissa's situation. The logical part of her brain (which sounded amazingly like Elizabeth) kept insisting Jessica wasn't responsible, laying out all sorts of facts and detailed analysis to back her claim. But the emotional section of her brain (the larger part) still felt there was some sort of connection, no matter how removed it was.

"Jess? You okay?" Jeremy reached over and set his fingertips on her shoulder. "You know, we really don't have to get ice cream. We could do something else."

Jessica sat forward and smiled. "No, no. I love ice cream. Ice cream is great." She winced inwardly. Her reply sounded like a lame cheer.

"You sure? You looked sort of distant there."

"Oh, I was just . . . listening to this song," Jessica improvised.

Okay. Get it together, girl. Here you are, out on the town with a wonderful guy, and all you can do is think about your problems. How warped is that? Did Elizabeth twist your hair so much it bored into your skull?

As they walked into the heavily air-conditioned interior of Scooper Duper's, Jessica quickly checked her reflection in the glass door. One of the hair balls had unraveled somewhat and was hanging down the right side of her face like a lifeless snake. Great. How was she supposed to feel charming with limp hair?

"Hey, Jeremy?" She playfully twirled the strand around her finger. "I'm going to the rest room. Would you mind ordering for me?"

"No problem," Jeremy answered, surveying the menu. "What's your poison?"

"Let's see. A double scoop of chocolate-chip cookie dough with little sprinkles of . . . *Will*."

84

Jessica's heart stopped. It couldn't be happening. But it was. Standing right in front of her at the cash register was the unmistakable back view of Will Simmons. She recognized the broad shoulders, the left-fingers-in-front-pocket slouch, the boyish waves of sandy hair looping over the back of his baseball cap.

No! Why now? Just when I decided to let it go and have fun.

She briefly considered diving under one of the pink plastic tablecloths, but it was too late. Will turned around, brown paper sack in hand, and came chest to face with Jessica. A startled expression seized his features, and he stopped dead in his tracks.

"Jessica!" he exclaimed.

"Will. Uh . . . hi," she stammered. "What are you doing here?"

"Getting some ice cream." He held up the sack.

Duh. What did she think he was doing? Getting a pedicure?

"It's for Melissa," he added.

"Oh." Jessica's heart flinched again. "That's nice. How is she doing?"

"She's fine," Will answered a bit too quickly.

Will kept glancing from her to a spot off to her right, and Jessica suddenly became aware of Jeremy's presence beside her.

"Oh. I'm sorry," Jessica said with an awkward giggle. "Will, this is Jeremy. Jeremy, this is—"

"We know each other," Jeremy cut her off abruptly.

They know each other? Oh God. Just how well did *they know each other?* Suddenly the tension seemed as thick as hot fudge.

"Hey, Aames," Will greeted him curtly.

Jessica glanced back and forth at each of their stony faces. She could feel the sweat dripping down her back, gluing her lace coverlet to her skin. *How does ice cream stay solid in this place?* she wondered.

"Well . . . see ya," Will mumbled, ambling past them.

Jeremy made no reply.

"See ya," Jessica echoed. She watched as he strode out the door and into the evening haze.

A shiver passed through Jessica, and she suddenly felt weak, drained.

Will must blame her for what happened to Melissa. Why else would he be so blunt and sound so cold?

Jeremy Aames

Remember back when you were little and had all sorts of weird routines built into your daily life? You know the ones. Like my dad and I used to always say "pot roast" anytime we were upset about something. I have no idea how it started. It was like our own little curse word. "Pot roast!" I'd yell when I spilled my milk. "Pot roast!" Dad would shout when he stubbed his toe.

Then there was Bueller the Beagle. My aunt Louise gave him to me for my fourth birthday, and every morning I had breakfast with him. The stuffed animal would slouch on the seat next to me with an empty cereal bowl in front of him that I insisted was full of invisible doggie treats.

But the one I remember most clearly is our silly bedtime ritual. It was the same every night for years. Mom would smooth the covers around me while Dad read a story. Then we would do "best/worst." That consisted of each of us in turn relating the best part of our day and the worst.

Under the "best" category I always included things like Arnie Tolbert sharing his remote-control tractor with me, losing my front tooth during homeroom and scaring Tina Murchison with it, and learning to squirt water out of the hole where my tooth had been. "Worst" things were stuff like eating lima beans at dinner or having to watch reruns of that old live-action <u>Batman</u> show.

When I reached the ripe age of ten, I announced I didn't want to be tucked in anymore. But every night I'd still lie there in bed and consider the best and worst parts of my day. I still do.

Today my favorite moment was seeing Jessica as she opened the door of her house and smiled at me. It was like, I don't know . . . a sunrise.

There were several lousy parts of the day, but the worst had to be running into Will Simmons at the ice-cream shop and seeing the expression on Jess's face—and Will's. It made me nervous.

Something's going on there. I don't know what it is. But I don't like it.

CHAPTER

Rocky Road

When Will got to the hospital, Melissa was sitting up in her bed watching a rerun of *Friends*. She was alone.

Will's stomach tightened. For two days he'd been spared having to speak with her one-on-one. She was always either sleeping or mumbling incoherently or having long, emotional talks with her parents. Scratch that—with her father. Her mom had gone practically nonverbal since she'd found Melissa out cold in the bathroom on Sunday evening.

Then during history class today an office runner had delivered a note to Will from Melissa's mother that read, *Melissa's better! Come after football practice. Bring ice cream.*

He had been hoping the family would be here with her, but no such luck. Melissa had probably shooed them away somehow so she could have him to herself. Melissa, he knew, could make almost anyone do almost anything.

"Will!" She looked at him and smiled weakly. "Come on in." She hit the remote control to turn off the television and sat back expectantly.

"Hey, Liss." He managed a lukewarm grin as he strode up to her and quickly kissed her cheek. Then he busied himself with clearing off the nearby rolling table so she couldn't study his expression too closely.

"Rocky Road! My favorite," she said as he pulled the ice cream from the bag. She put her frail hand on top of his. "I love that I have a boyfriend who knows everything about me."

An invisible foot kicked Will in the gut. He wanted to remind her that he wasn't her boyfriend anymore, but there was no telling how she would react. Besides, she was right about one thing: He probably *did* know everything about Melissa—too much, in fact. It was a giant weight that pulled him down constantly. Because of it, he never felt separate from her. And lately all he wanted to do was shake off the burden and run free. Melissa's eyes bored into Will as he handed her a plastic spoon. He knew she was expecting him to say something.

"You look better," he said, settling into the nearby chair. "Fantastic, actually."

Melissa took a deep breath and smiled. "The doctors say I'm doing great," she said. "They didn't even complain when Gina and Cherie showed up after cheerleading with a box of Guido's pizza."

"Gina and Cherie stopped by?" he asked, watching Melissa closely. She was oddly happy for a person in her situation. Plus the times he'd seen her with her father, she'd been upset and subdued. Was this smiley thing just an act for him?

"Yeah. They updated me on all the school gossip," Melissa answered. "They told me everyone at school was worried about me. Well," she paused, glancing right at him, "maybe not *everyone*."

Will tried to freeze his casual expression. He knew Melissa was testing him, trying to see if her cloaked reference to Jessica would trigger some physical reflex. But he maintained his cool, staring at her vacantly as if she were discussing a change in weather conditions.

Eventually she glanced back down at her tray and shakily removed the lid to the ice-cream container. Will grimaced. She was still so weak.

"Almost all of my teachers are going to just let me skip assignments," Melissa said, spooning up a bite of Rocky Road. "Cherie told me Mr. Collins will even let me off the hook for a bad paper I handed in *last* week. But I don't know. I think I'll try to do all the work anyway. . . ."

As she talked, Will let himself think. Immediately his mind jumped to the image of Jessica standing side by side with Jeremy. She looked so gorgeous. And Aames had that freshly shaven, pressed-shirt look typical of an early dating play formation. The sight of them together made Will feel sick.

Why couldn't life be like football? On the field he was the master. He always had the option of handing off the ball, launching a perfect pass, or faking out his enemies and sneaking across their line of defense. And if he absolutely had to, he could run.

In his entire high-school career he'd only been sacked five times. Lately, off the field, he'd been hit over and over and over.

". . . and I'm supposed to take a couple of weeks off from school and see this therapist, but when I get back, the coach wants me right back on the squad. Physical activity is supposed to be good for me. . . ."

Melissa's face was gaining color as she chatted. She was talking as if nothing was wrong—as if she wasn't sitting in a hospital bed waiting for an IV to flush out the last remaining traces of the narcotics she'd swallowed.

He knew he should feel sorry for her, but he didn't. Anyone else who heard about Melissa's suicide attempt always sucked in their breath and gasped, "Oh my God! Poor Melissa!" But not Will. When Melissa's father called him with the news Sunday evening, his first reaction was pure anger—anger that she would go so far and hurt so many people, including herself. At the emergency room he had overheard the doctor telling Melissa's parents that she most likely didn't want to die, that it was only a cry for help. And Will knew the cry was meant for him.

And now here he was. Sitting at her bedside. Fetching ice cream.

It was clear that Melissa thought things were going to return to the way they used to be. But he couldn't let that happen, no matter what. He couldn't stand by and let her continue to torment Jessica, and he couldn't let her go back to manipulating him. He really cared for Melissa and wanted her to be safe, but he wasn't in love with her anymore. Maybe he never really was. Maybe what he thought was love was actually a feeling of fierce protectiveness.

Will knew what he needed. He needed out. He just couldn't handle the possessive choke hold she had on him—making him completely responsible for her state of mind. So what was he waiting for? Why didn't he just tell her it was over?

"So then Cherie starts flirting with this doctor, and I'm thinking, 'Yeah, right. Lots in common there—'"

"Hey, Liss," he blurted out suddenly. "There's something I need to talk to you about."

Melissa peered at him warily, slumping back against her pillows. "What is it, Will?" Her voice contained that slight edge—that subtle challenge that implied he better not say anything she didn't want to hear.

At that moment a large, red-haired nurse burst into the room.

"Time for a new IV," the woman sang out as she approached Melissa's bed.

Will shut his mouth and hung his head. Perfect timing.

"Aha! I see someone has been eating nonregulation food items." The nurse gestured toward Melissa's half-eaten pint of ice cream as she hooked a plastic bag of clear liquid onto the IV pole. "So that's why you didn't eat the lime Jell-O I brought you earlier."

Melissa shrugged meekly. "I had to eat it. It was a present from my boyfriend," she explained, nodding in Will's direction.

Boyfriend. The term stung Will like a giant scorpion. He slunk back in his chair, using the nurse's tall, stout frame as a shield against Melissa's stare.

"Oh? Boyfriend, huh?" the nurse repeated, shoving a thermometer into Melissa's mouth. "I tell you what, that's the best medicine. The patients who have people looking out for them get better in no time." She turned and grinned at Will.

He wanted to run out of the room, yell at the top of his lungs, bash his head against the wall—anything to avoid the major guilt trip he could feel himself about to embark on. But it was no use. A feeling of remorse was already tightening around his throat like a rough but familiar noose.

"Yep," the nurse went on, filling the awkward silence while waiting on Melissa's temperature. "Sometimes ending up in a place like this can show you who you can depend on. The people who stop by and stick by your side, *they're* the ones who really care."

The electronic thermometer beeped, and the nurse slipped it out of Melissa's mouth to read it. Will saw Melissa swallow hard and press her fingers against her throat. Obviously it was still tender from the tubes. Then as the nurse took Melissa's blood pressure and pulse, he couldn't help but notice how thin Melissa's wrist and arm looked.

"All righty. Here you go," said the nurse as she plugged the new IV bag into the transparent tube sticking out of Melissa's right hand. She jiggled it and tapped it a couple of times to get the fluid moving, then added fresh tape to hold down the needle.

Melissa stared down at her IV, her forehead creasing. "When will they unhook me from this thing?" she asked.

The nurse smiled warmly and patted the top of Melissa's head. "Don't worry, honey. It won't be long."

Will felt like a swamp rat. How could he even think about unloading everything on Melissa now? For all he knew, she couldn't even handle something like that physically. A vision of doctors and nurses racing into her room with resuscitation machines ran through his mind.

"Well, you two take care now," the nurse chirped before exiting the room. "Enjoy that ice cream!"

As soon as the door was completely closed, Melissa fixed a cautious gaze on Will. "What was it you wanted to tell me?" she asked.

"Nothing," he mumbled. "Just that . . . it's good to see you looking so much better."

She smiled. "Thanks. It's because you're here, you know."

Will forced a grin while his insides ripped into shreds.

Melissa tried to scoop out another spoonful of ice cream, but her movements strained at her freshly taped IV hand.

"Here," Will said, stepping forward. "Let me." He took the spoon and lifted out a small mound of ice cream and marshmallow, depositing it into Melissa's mouth.

She smiled gratefully, fixing him with a tender gaze as she chewed and swallowed. "Thanks," she whispered.

"Don't mention it," he replied. *It's what I'm here for.*

Please be home. Please be home, Jessica chanted to herself as she counted the distant rings on the other end of the phone line. Three . . . four . . .

When she woke up Wednesday, Jessica had mentally replayed the events of the previous evening. Time, distance, and a good night's sleep helped her see everything in a new, less nerve-racked frame of mind. And it made her feel horrible.

97

How could she have been so awful to Jeremy? He'd planned such a wonderful night out and all she could do was obsess about Will and Melissa. And later, when they ran into Will, she'd lost any threads of sanity she had left. She'd been spacey for the rest of the night. Jeremy probably thought she had split personalities—and both of them awful.

Five rings . . . six rings . . . *Come on! Answer!*

Obviously Will hated her. There was that. But why did she care? And why was she punishing Jeremy? The one person outside of her family who'd been decent to her throughout this mess? She'd make it up to him. She had to.

Seven rings . . . eight rings . . . *What is going on?* It was only seven-thirty. Jeremy had to be awake. And it was too soon for him to have left for school.

Finally, just as Jessica was about to hang up, she heard the *click* of someone picking up the line.

"Hello?" *Jeremy!*

"Hey! It's Jessica."

"Jessica?" He sounded out of breath.

"I'm sorry. Did I wake you?" she asked.

"No. We have the ringers off upstairs so Dad can rest," Jeremy said. "I didn't hear the phone until I was headed down for breakfast. So what's up?"

Jessica bit her lip. "Not much. I just feel really bad about last night."

"Hey, I'm the one that took you out on another nondate," he said softly. "I think I'm cursed."

Jessica laughed. "Well, you may be cursed, but *I* was totally out of it all night. And I want to make it up to you."

"Oh? What did you have in mind?" Jeremy asked.

"How about you come over for dinner tonight around seven?" Jessica suggested. "I'll cook."

"Sounds great," Jeremy answered.

"You've obviously never been subjected to my cooking," Jessica said.

"I've seen you burn an espresso now and then. I've been properly warned," Jeremy joked.

"Good point. Dinner will have to be a family thing, but maybe we could go for a walk or something after?"

"Sounds great," Jeremy said. "I'll be there at seven."

"See you then!"

Jessica hung up the phone and danced around her bedroom in her nightshirt.

She did it! He was coming! It was going to be just what they needed. They'd get to sit down with Mom and Dad—and maybe Elizabeth—eat a home-cooked meal, have wonderful conversation, and maybe go for an evening stroll. There was so much to do, she wasn't sure where to start.

Of course, she should probably go tell everyone else he was coming.

"So luckily Mr. Fowler has a late meeting, Mrs. Fowler is going to some Junior League banquet, and

Lila is doing whatever with whoever." Jessica down-shifted the Jeep and careened around a corner, creating a sudden centrifugal force that made everything lean left.

"Whomever," Elizabeth corrected, grabbing hold of the passenger door handle. A split second later she was thrown backward in her seat as Jessica screeched to a halt for a red light. Elizabeth wondered why the air bags didn't engage.

Her sister's reckless driving almost made Elizabeth regret getting into the car—almost, but not quite. Actually, when Jessica had bounced up to her between classes and asked if she wanted to join their family and Jeremy for dinner, Elizabeth was totally relieved. She just couldn't face another dull, noiseless night at the Sandborns'.

She thought it ironic that at her own house, she used to constantly complain that it was too loud to concentrate. At the Sandborns' it was just the opposite. For them everyone cloistering themselves in their respective bedrooms for hours at a time seemed to be the status quo. It was quieter, yes, but eerily so. Elizabeth sometimes strained to hear evidence of another living soul within the house—especially sounds of the Conner variety.

"So, how was practice?" Elizabeth asked, hoping to keep her mind off Conner.

"I didn't have practice today," Jessica answered. "Tia and I tried out for the play."

"You did?" Elizabeth asked. "I thought you weren't going to do it this year."

"Yeah, well, Tia was pretty persuasive," Jessica said, tossing back her hair.

"She whined in your ear until you said yes?" Elizabeth asked, grinning.

"Man, that girl can be annoying when she wants to be," Jessica said with a laugh. "But I'm glad I did it. It might actually be fun if we get parts. And maybe none of the jocks who seem to enjoy torturing me so much will show up. They probably hate the drama club anyway."

Elizabeth looked at her hands. "Was Maria there?"

"No," Jessica said, pulling to a stop at an intersection. "And she was really bitchy to Tia about it the other day too. Like she was too good for it or something."

"Cut her some slack," Elizabeth said. "She did just have her best friend stab her in the back."

Jessica frowned. "No progress there, huh?" she asked.

"No progress," Elizabeth said glumly.

"I'm sorry, Liz," Jessica said. Just then the light turned green and Jessica stomped on the accelerator. Elizabeth's hair clip jabbed into her scalp as she bounced violently off the headrest.

"Jess!" Instinctively Elizabeth's foot pressed against an invisible brake pedal. "Why are you driving so fast? If you keep taking those corners at forty miles an hour, they'll be using a giant can opener to get us out of the car!"

"Sorry," Jessica mumbled, easing off the gas. "I guess I'm just nervous."

"About tonight?"

Jessica nodded. "There's so much to do. I really appreciate you coming home tonight to help me out."

"Hey, no problem. It's not like I'm missing out on anything else," Elizabeth said bitterly.

Jessica narrowed her eyes at Elizabeth and opened her mouth to speak, but Elizabeth cut her off.

"Besides," she said in a more cheerful tone. "Jessica Wakefield cooking dinner? *This* I had to see."

"Yeah," Jessica said with a laugh. "I can hardly believe it myself."

Elizabeth exhaled in relief, glad Jessica hadn't asked about her comment. Jessica was far too excited about her date, and Elizabeth didn't want to ruin that with a deep discussion. It had been ages since Elizabeth had seen her sister this animated. Thank God for Jeremy. Lately he'd been like a happy drug for Jessica. Too bad Elizabeth's own love life was such a downer right now or she could really share in the joy.

"Mom and Dad are going to love Jeremy. Don't you think?" Jessica asked.

"Yeah," Elizabeth agreed, trying to match Jessica's enthusiasm. "So, what time is he coming over?"

"Seven."

"Uh . . . Jess." Elizabeth pointed to the clock on the dashboard. "It's almost five-thirty."

"What? Is that not enough time?" Jessica's face creased with worry.

"How, exactly, are you going to shower, get ready, and make dinner in an hour and a half?" Elizabeth asked.

Jessica shrugged. "I don't know. It's just a cozy little dinner for five people. I figure that won't take too long to throw together. Right?"

Elizabeth pointed to the road ahead. "You better step on it," she said ominously.

Jessica Wakefield

To-Do List for Big Dinner with Jeremy

- Get Elizabeth to do my hair in a conservative, risk-free French braid this time.

- Hide that ugly porcelain dog the Fowlers keep in the sitting room.

- Make sure Dad's wearing a decent tie — especially not the blue one with little Tasmanian devils all over it.

- Plead with Mom not to tell the story about when I peed my pants on Santa's lap.

- Make sure Jeremy sits across from me so I can read his expressions.

- No matter what, <u>don't</u> <u>think</u> <u>about</u> <u>Will</u> <u>and</u> <u>Melissa</u>!

"What's that stuff?" Jessica asked, pointing to the big pot Luisa was stirring.

"Tortilla soup," Luisa replied impatiently.

"And what's in the oven?" Jessica asked, pulling the oven door open and squinting. "Chili cheese something?"

"*Chilaquiles*," Luisa corrected. "*Chi-la-qui-les*."

"*Chi . . .* ," Jessica began.

"Just call it enchilada pie, Miss Wakefield," Mrs. Pervis suggested. "That's a little easier."

"Great. Enchilada pie. Soup. Rice. Black beans." Jessica circled the kitchen, listing the menu items. "Now, are you sure everything will be ready on time?"

Mrs. Pervis and Luisa stole quick, irritated glances at each other. Jessica knew she'd asked that question already. A few times, actually. But it didn't hurt to ask it again. For all she knew, a major culinary setback might have occurred in the last five minutes.

"Yes, Miss Wakefield," Mrs. Pervis replied calmly. "It'll all be ready on time."

"Great!" Jessica headed toward the door. "Thank you *so* much. I really appreciate you doing all this. It's not going to be too spicy, will it?"

Jessica thought she saw Mrs. Pervis eye a nearby butcher knife longingly, but she couldn't be sure.

"No, Miss Wakefield. It won't be too spicy," Mrs. Pervis said. She smiled without raising the corners of her mouth—as if she were baring her teeth at Jessica.

"Okay." Jessica backed through the kitchen door, nervously surveying the activities one last time. "Thanks again!"

As soon as the door shut behind her, Jessica's smile faded. She checked her watch. Only ten minutes to go before Jeremy arrived. Where were her parents? Where was Elizabeth? Why wasn't the food ready yet?

All right. Just chill, Jessica told herself. *One thing at a time.*

She stepped out into the dining room and circled the large mahogany table that had already been set for dinner, appraising the lace tablecloth and straightening the place settings until everything was geometrically aligned. Then she glanced at the centerpiece and frowned. Mrs. Pervis had arranged a spray of strange, exotic-looking flowers. Jessica reached up and pulled a few of the twisty-looking sticks out of the arrangement. It helped, but the bouquet still had a wild, unruly look to it.

Speaking of which . . . Jessica trotted into the foyer to check her reflection in the big, beveled mirror. Luckily the steam from the kitchen hadn't messed up her makeup, but her hair did look a little droopy.

"Elizabeth?" she called out, heading toward the stairwell. "Elizabeth? Plug the curling iron back in. My hair's falling."

"What?" came Elizabeth's muffled voice from upstairs.

Jessica cupped her hands over her mouth and shouted, "I said my hair is falling!"

"Do I hear Chicken Little out there?" Jessica's father poked his head out of the nearby study.

Jessica rolled her eyes. "Dad, you're such a geek."

"But a cute geek," her father said, smiling.

"All right. I'll give you cute," Jessica said, quickly surveying his attire. Beige pants, powder blue shirt, loafers, and navy cardigan. A little too Mr. Rogersish, but she'd prefer that to his plaid golfing pants or the Not Dead Yet T-shirt he got for his fortieth birthday.

"What's all this shouting I hear?" Jessica's mother asked, coming down the stairs.

Jessica smiled. Her mom was wearing the rose-colored suit she'd worn to work that day and looked perfect as always. It was always clear to Jessica where she'd inherited her good taste.

"Nothing," Jessica whined. "Just that there's only a few minutes until Jeremy gets here, and my hair's going flat, and the flowers are too spiky, and the food is probably too spicy for anyone with a tongue."

Her mother and father looked at each other and grinned.

"I saw that!" Jessica protested. "I know you think I'm just obsessing, but I'm not. I only want everything to be perfect tonight. Just one night. Is that too much to ask?"

Mrs. Wakefield walked up to Jessica and put a reassuring arm around her shoulders. "Calm down, sweetheart. Everything *is* perfect. Besides, if this guy is as special as you say he is, he won't be offended by spiky flowers or limp hair."

"Oh, no!" Jessica whined, patting her hands over her head. "So my hair really *is* awful, isn't it? I knew it! Elizabeth! *Elizabeth!*"

"What?" Elizabeth appeared at the top of the stairs. "What's wrong?"

"I need to fix my hair again. Just look at it! My curls are wilting."

"Are you done *cooking* already?" Elizabeth said, arching an eyebrow.

"Hey, at least I know when I'm in over my head," Jessica said. "I delegated. Can we get back to the hair at hand?"

Elizabeth walked down the stairs and squinted at Jessica's hairdo. Then she turned and grinned at her mother and father. "She's obsessing, isn't she?"

"I am not!" Jessica's panic was starting to reach critical levels.

"Come with me." Elizabeth grabbed Jessica's arm and steered her back toward the foyer mirror. Then she licked her thumb and forefinger and began fluffing up the corkscrewlike tendrils that framed Jessica's face. "Now, see?" she said when she'd finished. "You're flawless. If your hair had any more body, we'd have to put a girdle on it."

"But what about—"

"Uh-uh. Stop." Elizabeth held up a hand. "Everything has been taken care of."

"But—"

"Stop," Elizabeth repeated, smiling. "Now quit worrying. You know it'll just cause your makeup to crack."

"You're really enjoying this, aren't you?" Jessica frowned at her sister. "You and Mom and Dad think this whole thing is funny."

"You know, it's been a long time since your last big spoiled-brat act," Elizabeth said affectionately. "It's almost like you're your old self again."

"Who are you calling spoiled, Miss Know-it-all?" Jessica retorted, a grin creeping onto her face.

But Elizabeth was right—as usual. She *did* feel like her old self again for the first time in a long, long while. Could it be that simple? Here she was bickering with her sister, freaking out about her hair, and waiting impatiently for a date to show up—just like old times. Somehow she'd survived the emotional shakedown of the past few weeks. She was still here.

"Girls, it's almost seven o'clock." Jessica's mom walked up behind them. "Let's have a seat and wait for our guest to arrive."

"You ready?" Elizabeth asked Jessica softly.

"Yes," Jessica replied, nodding resolutely. She hooked her arm through her sister's, and they followed their mother to the nearby sitting room.

Tonight was going to be perfect, Jessica thought happily. She and Jeremy would finally have the evening they'd been wanting.

After all, third time's the charm, right?

Elizabeth Wakefield

Mr. Quigley's Freestyle Writing Assignment

Write about anything that comes to mind? Hmmm. Not sure I can fill that order. Not today. The thing is, I'm tired of words. Words are useless. They're never precise enough to describe real thoughts and emotions.

Take <u>love</u>, for instance. That word is thrown around all the time. We "love" our parents, our dog, chocolate-chip ice cream, our country, and our boyfriend. But what exactly does it mean? How can one monosyllabic term accurately convey the whirlpool of chemical activity going on in our brains? It just doesn't cut it.

That's why I don't buy into that whole paperback-romance version of "love." You know the ones I'm talking about? The covers always show big-haired, busty women with their bodices half undone swooning in the arms of a shirtless Neanderthal. In my view, those stories do more to undermine relationships than romanticize them. Because of them girls expect to find chivalrous Fabio look-alikes who will rescue them from their dull existences wearing nothing but leather breeches.

Nothing is ever that perfect or easy. In reality people get zits and say dumb things and have names like Tim and Becky instead of Chase and Sharna. Real relationships take patience and sacrifice and lots of communication—if you actually communicate, that is.

See, that's the catch. If you need to communicate to make things work, then you need to use words. And words, like I said, are useless. Therefore it cannot be done.

And this entire paper is a waste too.

CHAPTER 7
Strike Three

"Hello, Mr. Wakefield. Nice to meet you." Jeremy stuck his arm into the air and shook hands with an imaginary person, someone with the size and disposition of Hulk Hogan—except possibly meaner.

That's how Jeremy pictured Jessica's father. Even if Mr. Wakefield didn't have the intimidating stature, Jeremy figured any man with two beautiful daughters had to have mastered the art of bullying prospective boyfriends.

"Gun collection? Sure, Mr. Wakefield, I'd love to see it," Jeremy said to his closet door as he finished tucking in his button-down shirt. "No, I had no idea you'd been a Green Beret. How fascinating."

When Jessica asked him to join her family for dinner, Jeremy had been flattered and relieved. After the way their previous two attempts at a date had gone, he was worried she'd written him off completely. But as excited as he was to finally have a nice evening with her, he was also extremely nervous about being put through the old "meet-the-folks" trial.

Jeremy walked over to his dresser and ran a

comb through his hair, which was still damp from his recent shower. "Nice to meet you, sir," he said, studying his reflection as he talked.

After fixing his hair and checking his face to make sure all traces of grime from football practice were gone, Jeremy quickly glanced at his watch. Two minutes till seven.

"Good job, Aames," he grumbled. He'd been so hung up on making a good impression, and now he was going to be late. Jeremy grabbed his car keys and sped out the door, running headlong into his mother in the hallway.

"Oh, good! You're still here," she said, placing her hands on his shoulders. "Listen, I need to ask you a favor."

"Sorry, Mom. I'm kind of in a hurry." He slid past her and headed toward the stairwell.

"Jeremy, wait! I'm sorry, honey, but you have to stay here tonight."

"Huh?" Jeremy stopped in midstride and turned to face his mother's somber stare. A feeling of foreboding pressed down on him.

His mother crinkled up her brow apologetically. "I just got a call from work, and I have to go in right away. Unfortunately your father hasn't been feeling too well, and this evening he wouldn't eat any of his dinner. I really don't want him home alone with the girls. Can you please stay and keep them out of his hair?"

"But . . . but . . ." Jeremy's thoughts flipped back and forth between Jessica and his father like a fierce Ping-Pong match—only with Jeremy as the sure loser.

"I heard that!" Emma appeared in the doorway of her room, her bony arms folded across her chest. "I don't need a baby-sitter, Mom! I'm twelve! And I can watch Trisha all by myself."

As if on cue, Trisha suddenly pushed past Emma and bolted down the hallway, shrieking.

"Hey!" Emma yelled, running after her. "That's my bracelet! Give it back!"

The girls disappeared around the corner, their shouts and wails growing fainter as they ran down the stairs.

Jeremy and his mother exchanged knowing glances. "You're right," he mumbled. "I'll stay home and keep them away from Dad."

"I'm sorry, sweetheart," Mrs. Aames said, patting his arm consolingly. "I know you had plans, but I'm sure your friends will understand. Your father's health is more important."

He sighed slowly. "I know, Mom," he said. "It's okay." His personal life would just have to wait for the time being. Right now his duty was to see his father through this. As much as he wanted to race out of the house and drive over to Jessica's waiting smile, he couldn't let his family down. And as tough as it was for him, he knew things were even tougher on his dad.

"We couldn't get through this without you, you know," his mother whispered, her eyes liquid.

"It's all right, Mom," Jeremy said flatly.

"Call me if you need anything," Mrs. Aames said, and disappeared down the stairs.

For a long moment Jeremy stood there, thinking. Then he sighed pitifully and walked back into his room, snatching the cordless phone off his desk. He really, really didn't want to disappoint Jessica a third time. But he had no choice.

After the second ring Jessica's lilting voice met his ear. She sounded so cheerful and eager, he almost hung up.

"Hey, Jessica. It's Jeremy."

"Jeremy!" she sang out. "Wait a minute. Where are you?"

"I'm at home. Listen . . ." He shut his eyes tightly. "I can't come after all."

There was a brief pause on the other end.

"Oh," Jessica said softly.

"It's my dad. He hasn't been eating today, and Mom has to go in to work. I really need to stay here and keep an eye on him in case he gets worse and . . . Please tell your parents I'm really sorry," he said helplessly.

"It's okay, Jeremy. We all understand what you're dealing with," Jessica said.

"Thanks," Jeremy said. "So . . ."

"Listen," Jessica said, "I know this is going to

sound weird, but after everything that's happened . . . maybe—I don't know—maybe this just isn't supposed to happen. Maybe *we're* not supposed to happen. I mean, it's like the fates are against us or something."

"No! Don't say that! We'll get together. I promise!" Jeremy's mind raced. He couldn't let Jessica give up yet. All he needed was one solid chance. "How about Friday night? Do you have plans?"

"Uh . . . no."

"Good! Leave it open for me," Jeremy said. "I just . . . I just want to see you."

"In that case . . ."

"*This* time I promise it will work out." The determination behind his voice surprised even Jeremy. "How about dinner out somewhere? Maybe that new beachside Italian place?"

"Sounds great," she murmured. "But won't it be expensive?"

"I heard it's cheap but good," Jeremy said, mentally reviewing his last bank statement. "Besides, I saved up some money for a water-heater repair and then my mom found out it was under warranty."

"But Jeremy, I know you really need to—"

"Forget it," Jeremy said, smiling. "I'm allowed to have a little fun, right? For once I don't want to be stressed about money."

Jessica laughed. "Okay."

"All right, then. I'll pick you up at seven. If we crash and burn this time, you have permission to stand me up against a wall and throw knives at me."

"I'm sure that won't be necessary," she said, laughing. "I'll see you soon. Hope your father feels better."

"Thanks, Jess. Bye."

Jeremy hung up the phone and took his first deep breath in several minutes. Friday. He'd bought himself more time.

He wasn't one to see bad omens in things, but it did seem rather ominous that three dates in a row had fizzled. With anyone else he'd have already lost hope.

But Jessica was definitely worth the effort.

Elizabeth walked—or rolled, rather—through the Sandborns' foyer. Her stomach was stuffed with Mexican food, giving her all the energy of a garden slug.

As usual, the house was about as lively as a mausoleum. She figured everyone was off in his or her room, and for once that was just fine with her. All she wanted to do was get out of her skirt (which seemed dangerously close to bursting off her anyway), put on some old sweats, lie down, and listen to Sarah McLachlan over her headphones.

As she dragged herself up the stairs, each step seemed to groan beneath her weight. Elizabeth made a mental note to do one hundred sit-ups the next day—if she could manage to bend at the waist. She hadn't meant to eat so much at dinner, but the food was so good, and she had to do something to keep her mouth occupied anyway. Since Jeremy hadn't been able to show and Mom and Dad were trying to spare Jessica's feelings, they filled up the dinner conversation by interrogating Elizabeth on her life. Eating was the only way to throw them off.

Elizabeth hoisted herself off the last step and yawned gigantically. It wasn't even nine o'clock, but she suddenly had the urge to curl into a ball and sleep—perhaps hibernate through the next six months or so.

Suddenly Conner flung open his bedroom door and walked into the hall. He was slipping on his jacket as he walked and didn't even notice Elizabeth until they were face-to-face. Elizabeth stood and stared at him, her mouth still gaping open in midyawn. "Hey," he said. He sounded casual, but his eyes widened slightly before concentrating on the Berber carpeting.

"Hey," she echoed, her voice more breath than sound.

Elizabeth took in every minute detail of Conner's image—his fine, feathery lashes, the dampness on his lower lip, the way the muscles in his throat twitched slightly.

He was only inches away from her. All she needed to do was lift her hands and lean her body a few degrees forward. . . . But she stayed rooted in place—frozen stiff on the outside, a maelstrom of emotion on the inside.

"You're going out?" she asked quickly. *Good one, Elizabeth,* she scolded herself. *Real astute.*

"I'm meeting Andy," he said. "We're going to grab some pizza."

"Oh," she replied. Elizabeth waited for him to invite her along, but he didn't say anything more. "Well, I just ate," she explained. "I'm stuffed."

"Good for you," he said, one corner of his mouth lifted in a half smirk. Then his gaze turned back toward the stairwell behind her.

Stop him, her mind urged. *Don't let him go.*

She tilted herself into his field of vision. "So," she began brightly, but could think of nothing to follow it with. "Uh . . ."

Elizabeth wished her brain would conjure up a clever, irresistibly witty phrase, but at the moment it was far too occupied with thoughts of kissing Conner and far too busy mapping the contours of his face.

He met her gaze and smiled wryly.

She smiled back.

Then his arm raised up and reached around her.

For a split second every one of Elizabeth's nerves seemed to stretch toward that arm, waiting for it to descend and pull her toward him. Instead it stretched completely past her, and Conner settled his hand on the stairwell's sloping wood banister.

"Well . . . see ya," he said.

"Wait!" She quickly leaned to her left, blocking his path. "I, uh, I talked to Maria yesterday."

His smile disappeared, and he stared at her intensely. "How did it go?"

"It didn't, actually," she said dejectedly. "She won't listen to me."

Elizabeth watched as Conner's facial muscles relaxed. He almost looked relieved.

"I'm sorry, Elizabeth," he murmured. "Maybe she just needs . . . a little more time."

Time. There was that word again. Elizabeth was tired of everything needing so much time. She stared into Conner's deep green eyes, wanting desperately for him to take advantage of the "now" that they had.

"I need to go meet Andy," he said, sidestepping around her. Elizabeth felt as though she'd been stabbed.

"Conner!" His name escaped from her mouth before she realized it.

He stopped, but it took a moment for him to turn around again.

"How long are we going to have to avoid each other?" she asked, meeting his gaze.

This time his features softened into an expression of real, undeniable concern. "I thought you wanted to figure things out with Maria first," he said softly.

"I do, but—"

"I'm sorry," Conner interrupted. "I've really got to go. We'll talk about this soon. I promise."

And with that, Conner disappeared down the stairs and out the front door.

"Bye," Elizabeth mumbled to the space he left behind.

Elizabeth trudged into her room and sat down on the bed. As her body untensed, she felt strangely empty inside. *How can it be so easy for him?* she wondered. As much as she wanted to believe otherwise, Elizabeth couldn't help thinking that Conner *wanted* to stay away from her.

Suddenly she had an instinctive urge to call Maria and tell her about her guy troubles like she always did, letting Maria's talent for sorting through messes uncover a brilliant solution. But then she remembered. Maria wasn't there for her anymore. Not for anything.

And especially not this.

The phone was ringing on the desk in Will's bedroom.

He didn't want to answer it. He knew who it was. It was almost as if he could tell by the ring: demanding, yet even and persistent—never growing more shrill, but never stopping either.

Finally he sighed and picked it up. "Hello?"

"Will!" Sure enough, it was Melissa. "What took you so long to pick up?"

"I . . . uh . . . I just got out of the shower."

"Oh. Well, I just wanted to call and tell you good night." Her voice was low and smooth.

"Good night," he murmured. Will's inner radar switched on. Something was up. Something more than a good-night smooch over the phone receiver. Melissa was checking up on him.

"I have good news," she announced.

Here goes, thought Will. "What is it?"

"I'm being discharged tomorrow. The doctors say I'm well enough to go home. Isn't that great?"

Will plopped down on his bed. A rush of anxiety flooded through him, braiding his nerves. If she was coming home, she was stronger. That meant he could finally confront her.

"That's great, Liss. I can't wait." He purged all apprehension from his voice, knowing he had to say the right thing. "Do you need a ride home from the hospital?"

"No. You know how Mom is all concerned with playing the perfect mother. She's picking me up herself around noon. But you're going to come see me after practice, right?" Melissa asked.

"Of course." His hands were trembling. He knew he couldn't keep up the act much longer. "Hey, Liss. My dad's expecting a call on this line. I really should go."

"Okay. Well . . . good night," she purred. "I love you."

Will forced out the words. "Me too. Bye."

After he'd hung up, he fell back on his bed and threw his arm over his eyes. She would be home tomorrow. He couldn't put it off any longer. He had to tell her things were over between them. For good.

But if things were over, why did he feel like the nightmare was just beginning?

Maria Slater

<u>Why Books Are Better Than People</u>

1. They don't hide any secrets. You can look in the inside and learn everything there is to know.
2. They don't require anything from you except maybe an occasional dusting.
3. If you don't like them, you can return them without any hassle.
4. You don't have to get dressed up to spend an evening with a good book.
5. They may occasionally get misplaced, but they never leave you of their own accord.
6. If things get scary or start moving too fast, you can simply slam the cover shut.
7. The only pain they inflict are minor paper cuts or a slight crick in the neck.

8 Bylines

Thursday after school Elizabeth dragged herself down the main corridor to her locker, marveling at the level of activity around her. Everyone seemed way too chipper, and their pace seemed far too upbeat. Not a care in the world. Didn't they know people's hearts were breaking all around them? Didn't they realize there were more important things than sports and trips to the mall?

The hallway seemed narrower and dingier than she'd ever noticed before—and suffocatingly humid, the mayonnaise-colored walls pressing toward her. Elizabeth had the eerie sensation that she was marching through an ancient catacomb, never to see daylight again.

"I wish," she muttered.

It had *not* been a good day.

In creative-writing class she had caught Conner staring at her. She'd leaned over to fish her pocket thesaurus out of her book bag and suddenly felt his eyes on her, like two tingly tractor beams. Somehow she found the nerve to look up and smile at him, only when she did, he immediately looked away.

Elizabeth decided she couldn't handle it anymore. Things were getting way too weird. It was one thing for Conner to give her space, but not the galaxy-sized void that was between them now. She had wanted their relationship to slow down, but not stop altogether.

He had said they would talk about things, and she figured they'd finally get a chance after class. Unfortunately when the dismissal bell rang, Conner once again managed to beat her to the door and disappear, just as he had the day before, and the day before that, and the day before that. It seemed a violation of physics that he could maintain his slow, ultracool strut and still outrun her.

"Yeah, sure we'll talk," Elizabeth mumbled under her breath. "Like when? Graduation?"

For the rest of the day she searched for him in the hallways but never saw him. She did, however, see Maria a couple of times. Unfortunately Maria had pretended not to see Elizabeth.

Elizabeth was beginning to feel like a slime-covered creature in a really bad horror movie. Even the other students seemed to be rushing away from her as they raced down the corridor out of school. Did no one want to be near her?

"Elizabeth!" a cheery voice called out. "Elizabeth, come here!" Megan stood down the hall in the doorway to the *Oracle* office, waving at her frantically.

Okay, so Megan still loved her. That was something.

"It's here!" Megan shouted, a huge smile lighting her face.

"What's here?" Elizabeth asked, smiling back.

"The paper! Well, it's not *here*, here. It's actually at the printers. But it's ready for us to go get it. I can't wait! My first real article is in there. Right at the top of page four. You know? The one on new college entrance requirements?" She bounced around on her feet giddily.

Elizabeth smiled. She remembered how excited she was when her first article had been published. "Yeah. It's a great piece, Megan. Very well researched."

Megan beamed. "Thanks. So . . . do you think you could take me to pick up our copies? Mr. Collins said we could."

"Oh, but I don't have the Jeep today."

"That's okay. Conner was just here, and he gave me the keys to his car." Megan dangled a large wad of keys from her fingers. "He said he'd catch a ride with some friends."

"Conner was just here?" Elizabeth asked, trying to sound nonchalant.

"Yeah. I invited him to come with us, but he said he had stuff to do. Told me to save him a copy." Megan leaned in closer and lowered her voice. "Actually, I think he was just avoiding running into Maria."

Or me, Elizabeth thought glumly.

"So what do you say, Elizabeth? Will you take me?" Megan was all eyes.

Elizabeth stared at the jingling keys hanging from Megan's hand. She couldn't believe it. Conner wouldn't bring himself to talk to her, but he'd actually let her drive his treasured car? How bizarre was that?

"Sure," she said, grabbing the keys and clutching them tightly. "Let's go."

They merged into the river of students heading out into the sunshine. Elizabeth noticed the lift in Megan's walk and the excited smile that couldn't be rubbed off her face. Once again Elizabeth felt like a big, depressing blob next to her.

Maybe that was it—the secret to true happiness. Forget love and friendship gone awry. Maybe it was the little things that really mattered. Like weekends and Oreo cookies and seeing your name in print for the first time.

And Conner's smile . . .

And Conner's voice . . .

And the way Conner's brow crinkles up when he concentrates . . .

Elizabeth sighed sadly. It really hurt when the little things were taken away.

Maria entered the *Oracle* classroom cautiously, ready for the worst, but she was in luck. No

Elizabeth. A note scrawled on the blackboard said she and Megan had gone to pick up the papers at the printers.

Good, Maria thought. *That'll buy me some time.*

She sat down in one of the chairs close to the door, put her head down on the desk, and closed her eyes. Exhaustion set in, weighing down her body like hardening cement.

Maria had faced the last several days of school with unflappable composure. She simply scrunched all her bad feelings into a small ball and carried it around deep inside her—there it bounced around, upsetting her insides, but her exterior remained cool and calm. Unfortunately doing so demanded a huge amount of Maria's energy, and her power stores were quickly depleting. Every time she ran into Conner or Elizabeth in the hallways, it put another chink in her already weakening armor.

Maria let herself relax in the confines of the stiff desk as best as she could, hovering in a quasi-sleep state. Gradually all external sensory input disappeared. There was only the quiet murmur of her heart and the cool gusts of her breath against her wrist.

When she opened her eyes again, the room had already filled with *Oracle* staff members waiting for the editorial meeting to begin. Maria blinked her present surroundings back into view, stood slowly, and stretched out her arms. The staffers, who were sitting on and around the long tables in the center of the room, stopped chatting and watched her expectantly. As usual, it looked like she would have to run the meeting since Elizabeth was gone. No big surprise there.

"Look. It moves," Walt Tibbets remarked from his perch on the back counter.

"Good morning, sunshine," Wendy Chen sang out, her dark eyes glittering as she grinned. Maria grimaced. As always, Wendy was way too cheerful, especially today in her pink sweater and little rhinestone barrettes. "Are you feeling okay?" Wendy asked, leaning forward in her front-and-center seat. "You look a little out of it."

"I'm fine," Maria replied nonchalantly. "I just . . . didn't sleep well last night."

Her nap had been brief and shallow, but it was enough to make her drop her defenses. The look of concern on Wendy's face triggered a rush of self-pity. Maria quickly took a deep breath and blinked back the moisture in her eyes. Then she balled up all the emotional aches and pains and pushed them deep within her.

"All right, gang," she began, the picture of serenity, "time to list ideas for the next issue's articles. Anyone have suggestions?"

The room turned silent, everyone suddenly interested in the condition of their shoes or the petrified spit wads on the ceiling.

"Come on, guys. What's going on out there?" Maria gestured toward the hallway.

Walt glanced out the window behind him. "Hmmm. I think the janitors have switched brands of glass cleaner. Want me to go interview them?"

A few people laughed appreciatively. Maria glared. Editorial meetings were usually pretty playful in the beginning, but today she was in no mood for it.

Someone besides her had to be thinking business. She turned to Jen Graft, the perky sophomore-turned-fashion-editor. "What's your idea for the new fashion column?" she asked.

Jen's big, brown eyes swiveled upward as she thought, and she swung her long, brown hair behind the back of her chair. "I know!" she said suddenly. "How about an exposé on Mr. Rhodes's toupee? With an accompanying photo."

More laughter.

"Sounds like a great piece," Walt quipped. "Get it? A great 'piece.'"

Maria sighed wearily. This was obviously going to take all afternoon, and she needed to get home soon—before she crumbled completely. Before the tears started leaking out right here, in front of everyone.

"Come on, guys," she pleaded. "Doesn't anyone have a serious suggestion?"

Silence.

Maria threw up her hands in exasperation. "Think! There has to be some big news taking place at school."

There was another brief pause, and then Leslie Beck tentatively raised her hand.

"Yes?" Maria pounced.

"We could do a piece on Melissa Fox," Leslie suggested. A few other students nodded in agreement.

"Um . . . what specifically did you have in mind?" Maria asked.

"Well, I think we should just write about her suicide attempt and how she almost died and stuff," Leslie said, twisting one of her many black corkscrew curls around her finger.

Maria shook her head. "No. We can't do that."

"Why not?" Walt asked. "It's news. We're supposed to cover the big stories, and that's the biggest one so far this year."

"Yeah," Jen echoed, doodling on the front of her blue binder. "And Melissa's a cheerleader. She's supposed to be like a role model."

"You don't understand," Maria said evenly. "What happened to Melissa isn't news—it's a personal matter."

"What's the difference?" Walt snorted.

"For one thing, it didn't happen on campus. It happened at her home," Maria pointed out, pulling her patchwork cardigan tightly around her body. "Second, everyone already knows the story. And for another thing, it wouldn't be ethical to write about something like this. Think about her feelings."

"But that's not what newspapers do," Walt protested. He leaned back against the window and lifted his chin. "They don't think about hurting the president's feelings when they write an editorial or worry about making a movie star mad when they slam his movie." He glanced around at the rest of the students and nodded smugly.

"You're not talking about her job here," Maria retorted. "You're talking about her private life. Do you want to set standards for ourselves or not? Because if we print this story and call it 'news,' we're just like those scumbags who try to shock people in order to sell papers."

"But we don't—," Walt began.

"Why don't people ever think about how their actions might hurt someone before they actually do things?" Maria cut him off, her voice now a full octave higher and several decibels louder. "All anybody cares about is getting what they want, no matter who they might step on along the way. It's disgusting!"

She spat out the last words with the intensity of an exploding grenade.

"Uh . . . okay." Walt's eyes were wide and wary. "Maybe you're right."

A sudden movement from behind startled Maria. She whirled around and saw Elizabeth and Megan standing in the doorway, carrying huge stacks of papers. A look of pain contorted Elizabeth's delicate features.

Quiet tension settled over the room like smoke from a recent bomb blast.

"Um . . . papers, anyone?" Megan called.

Elizabeth somehow found the presence of mind to set down the tower of papers teetering in her arms. Then she quietly slunk to the back of the room while the others swooped down on the stack, eagerly snatching up copies and flipping through the pages.

"Whoa. The features spread looks so cool!" she heard Jen Graft exclaim.

"Yeah, and the pictures didn't print all grainy this time," someone else added.

Walt Tibbets flashed her a thumbs-up. "Great job, Elizabeth. This is our best issue so far."

Elizabeth forced a smile, but she felt no pride. She couldn't take any credit for the issue since she had ditched so many meetings. Maria was the one who had pulled it off. But Elizabeth had the editorship, so technically it would count as her achievement. Yet another way she'd robbed her friend.

"You guys made this edition good," Elizabeth ventured. No response.

She knew Maria's fiery speech had been about her. The reference was indirect, but it definitely hit the mark. Maria's words had pierced her flesh and burrowed inside her, where they continued to throb intensely. "Scumbags," "no matter who they step on along the way," "disgusting." That was how Elizabeth felt, all right. Ugly and sneaky and in constant need of a shower.

Elizabeth watched as Maria bustled about, posting articles on the assignment board, answering questions, and counting out stacks of the paper for homeroom delivery the next day. As usual, she had completely reverted back to her stoic self—without any trace of her recent blowup.

"Hey, Elizabeth? Could I ask you for a favor?" Megan suddenly appeared beside her, a copy of the paper rustling in her hands.

"Sure. What is it?" Elizabeth said, sounding tired.

"Do you think you could drive me over to the country club?" Megan asked, scrunching up her nose shyly. "I know it sounds dumb, but I really want to surprise my mom with this. She's gonna freak."

"Of course," Elizabeth replied, smiling. "And no, it doesn't sound dumb." She leaned closer to Megan and lowered her voice. "Do you know my parents actually framed my first article?"

"Really?"

"No lie! It's on the wall in my dad's study. Or . . . it was. Before the earthquake." Elizabeth frowned, a sad nostalgia adding another layer to her misery. She quickly shook her head. "Anyway, I think it's a great idea, surprising your mom. Just give me a sec and we'll

135

go. I want to talk to Maria about something first."

"Okay," Megan said cheerfully. "But be careful. She's in a bad mood."

No kidding, Elizabeth thought as she walked over to the table where Maria sat sorting papers. She moved slowly and quietly, afraid Maria might run off if she caught wind of her.

Maria's head snapped up the minute Elizabeth came into range. A stricken expression breezed across her face and then was gone, replaced by an indifferent stare.

"Listen, Maria," Elizabeth began casually, "I overheard your little talk about . . . integrity, and I just want to say that you're right. Everything you said was right." She met Maria's eyes with an earnest, pleading look.

"Well, I'm glad to hear that," Maria said, standing abruptly.

"You are?" Elizabeth felt her heart skip.

"Yes," Maria continued, shouldering her book bag. "I'm thrilled you agree with my opinions on journalism ethics. It'll make our working relationship go much more smoothly." She headed toward the doorway. "Now, if you'll excuse me. I have to go home."

"But . . ." Elizabeth's face fell. "But I meant . . ."

It was too late. With a flounce of black curls Maria turned and went out. And so did Elizabeth's last flicker of hope.

Megan Sandborn

Once when I was little, my mother asked me what I wanted to be when I grew up. At that time my life was centered around fairy tales and Barbie dolls, so I told her I wanted to be a princess.

Mom freaked. She said no way, that she used to want to be a princess too, but look where it got her—no job skills and two failed marriages. "Pick something else," she told me. "Anything that doesn't require marrying a handsome prince."

I had no idea what else I could be. At first I toyed with the idea of becoming a professional ice-skater like Michelle Kwan, but a few intimate collisions between the ice rink and my rear end cured me of that. I even tried learning guitar from Conner and quickly learned his talent comes from the McDermott side.

Then one day we rented the movie <u>Superman.</u> It sort of changed my life.

While my friend Tracy was drooling over Christopher Reeve's pecs, I was studying the Lois Lane character. She was so together—independent, tough, gorgeous. And her job looked so cool. I loved the way she got to nose around in everyone's business and was always where the action was. Right then and there I decided to be a roving reporter just like her.

And now I'm on my way! My first full-length article will soon be circulating among the students at Sweet Valley High. People will actually be reading what I wrote, maybe even talking about it. Sooner or later they might even start to recognize my name!

I'll be Sweet Valley's answer to Lois Lane! Okay, so I may not be gorgeous or tough. And there's no Man of Steel swooping out of the sky to carry me to his secret ice castle. But I've got my byline.

And I didn't have to kiss any frogs to get it.

CHAPTER

Rude Awakening

Megan directed Elizabeth to the Valley Stream country club, a white stucco compound nestled between two gently sloping hills on the edge of town. Elizabeth pulled Conner's vintage Mustang into the parking lot in between a gold-colored Mercedes and some foreign-looking sports car with a space-age design.

By the time Elizabeth locked her door, Megan had already hopped out of the car and was heading up the stone walkway toward the pool. Elizabeth had to jog to catch up with her.

"Thanks so much for bringing me, Elizabeth," Megan said, reaching over to grab Elizabeth's wrist. "Mom's going to be so psyched. I've never been all that good at anything before this."

Elizabeth smiled. "You're a natural, Megan. I bet you'll be one of the top editors next year."

"You think so?" Megan's face glowed.

"Definitely," Elizabeth said, letting Megan's enthusiasm lift her spirits a bit.

"Could you maybe say that in front of my

mom?" Megan crinkled up her brow, just like Conner was always doing. Only on Megan it looked bashful instead of brooding.

"Sure," Elizabeth replied, laughing. "You know, we should have brought more than one copy of the paper with us. Your mom's probably going to want to hand it out to all her club friends."

Megan grinned.

They reached the top of the walkway and stepped onto the Mexican tile of the outdoor terrace. The club's large, lima-bean-shaped pool glimmered in front of them. Megan scanned the crowd of iced-tea-sipping club members and pointed to the opposite end of the terrace. "I think I see her," she said excitedly, then turned and rushed toward the far side of the pool.

Elizabeth followed Megan's bouncing figure to a white lounge chair that was practically hidden behind a couple of large potted trees. Mrs. Sandborn lay on top of it, her sunglassed face pointed toward the descending sun.

"Mom?" Megan said, placing her hands with the copy of the paper in them behind her back.

Mrs. Sandborn didn't respond.

"Mom?" Megan called louder.

Elizabeth squinted at Mrs. Sandborn's sprawled form. Her arms were hanging down at her sides, fingers grazing the patio tiles. The brightly colored skirt she had wrapped around her swimsuit was bunched awkwardly. "Uh, Megan?" Elizabeth whispered. "I think she's asleep."

Megan knelt down next to her mother and nudged her gently. "Mom? Mom, wake up. It's Megan."

Mrs. Sandborn's head only lolled to the side and her sunglasses slipped to the tile.

"Wow. She's really out," Elizabeth remarked slowly. Something struck her as being very wrong.

Megan frowned. "I hope she put on lots of sunblock," she said softly. "She hates it when she gets a sunburn."

Handing her copy of the *Oracle* to Elizabeth, Megan grabbed her mother's shoulders with both hands and shook her briefly. "Wake up, Mom. Mom? Mom!"

"Megan?" Mrs. Sandborn's eyes popped open. She glanced around her quickly, finally focusing on her daughter. "He-ey. Aren't you supposed to be in school?" she said, squinting.

Megan and Elizabeth exchanged startled glances.

"Mom. It's almost five o'clock," Megan explained.

"What?" Mrs. Sandborn shouted. She tried to sit up straight but lost her balance and grabbed onto the chair's hand rest. She paused for a moment and closed her eyes, clutching the chair. Then she belched quietly and lay back down, holding her hand over her eyes.

All color seemed to drain out of Megan's face.

141

"Mom, are you all right?" she asked meekly.

"I'm *fine*," Mrs. Sandborn said through clenched teeth.

Elizabeth's heart jumped at her tone, and she felt Megan stiffen next to her. What was going on?

"What are you two doing here?" Mrs. Sandborn said, covering her whole face with both hands. "Can't I have five seconds of peace? Five seconds without everyone in my face?"

"Mom, I'm sorry, I—" Megan teared up and wrapped her arms around her stomach.

"Oh, don't start crying now," Mrs. Sandborn spat. She swung her legs over the side of the chair and kicked over a martini glass. The olive rolled out onto the tiles as Mrs. Sandborn stood, wavered, and clutched Elizabeth's forearm for support. Elizabeth's heart dropped as the pieces started to fall into place. Mrs. Sandborn had been drinking.

"You're making a scene," Mrs. Sandborn told Megan.

That was when Elizabeth smelled her breath. Her stomach squeezed tightly, and she wrapped an arm around Mrs. Sandborn's back. "I think we should get you home," she said.

"Oh! Are you the new rescue wagon?" Mrs. Sandborn shouted, pushing away from Elizabeth. A few guests around the pool turned to stare. "You aren't even a member of this family," Mrs. Sandborn spat. She teetered again, and Elizabeth reached out to steady her. This time Mrs. Sandborn didn't move away. She leaned all her weight against Elizabeth's side.

Elizabeth was frightened. She'd never had to deal with anyone this trashed. Especially not an adult. She glanced over at Megan, who seemed frozen with shock and embarrassment. Elizabeth had to get them all out of here immediately.

"C'mon, Mrs. Sandborn. We're outta here," Elizabeth said, holding the woman's arm.

Mrs. Sandborn looked Elizabeth directly in the eye, her own eyes impossibly watery. "Okay," she said quietly.

Megan walked around to her mother's free side, and Mrs. Sandborn smiled weakly at her daughter. Together the three of them stumbled across the terrace, Megan and Elizabeth struggling under Mrs. Sandborn's near deadweight. Just outside the gate a prim-looking man in a suit approached from the direction of the clubhouse.

"Your mother is heading home, I presume?" he asked Megan. Mrs. Sandborn let out a bitter laugh.

"Yes. We're leaving right now, Mr. Pierson," Megan replied softly, clutching her mother's arm.

"Good." Mr. Pierson nodded briskly. "I'm sorry to say that your mother cannot return. I'm afraid she is no longer welcome at this club. We'll be sending her a letter rescinding her membership."

Megan stared at the man disbelievingly, then

lowered her gaze to the ground. Elizabeth tightened her grip on Mrs. Sandborn, whose head was starting to droop sleepily.

Mr. Pierson softened his voice. "I am sorry. We have given her several warnings, but unfortunately she chose to ignore them. This will have to be her last visit."

"I understand," Megan mumbled.

By the time they reached Conner's car, Mrs. Sandborn was mumbling incoherently and unable to stand. Elizabeth held her up while Megan opened the doors. Together they managed to lower her into the backseat.

As Elizabeth drove past the large concrete-and-cast-iron sign at the club's front entrance, fragments of the previous few weeks whirled through her mind. Mrs. Sandborn's late nights and even later mornings, her lengthy naps, her breath mints, the broken glasses . . .

Conner's mother was an alcoholic. Elizabeth couldn't believe she'd been living in the house this whole time and hadn't suspected a thing.

Elizabeth glanced over at Megan, who sat staring out the passenger-side window, her forehead pressed against the glass. Poor Megan. What could she say to her? What must she be feeling?

And Conner. Elizabeth remembered all the times he protected his mother's privacy, made excuses for her behavior, or went to pick her up somewhere because she had "car trouble." No wonder he was so closed off. But how could he be dealing with it all himself?

As Elizabeth gripped the steering wheel and stared grimly out at the winding road ahead, one thing was perfectly, heartrendingly clear—Conner had gone to serious lengths to keep this secret from her. Tears welled up in Elizabeth's eyes as a sickening realization pressed against her chest.

Conner didn't trust her enough to let her in.

"Will!" Mrs. Fox smiled and opened the door wide to let him in.

"Is Melissa in her room?" Will asked.

"Yes." Mrs. Fox sighed. "She's supposed to be resting, but I'm sure she's up and about. You know as well as I do that she never listens to me."

Will tried to return her grin, but he was too heavy with guilt. He nodded toward the stairs. "Is it all right if I go up?"

Mrs. Fox placed her hand against Will's back and led him away from the stairs. "Let's talk for a moment first," she said in a low whisper.

A line of sweat instantly broke out along Will's forehead. What could she possibly want to talk to him about?

She cast a look toward the stairs and then fixed her weary gaze on Will. "I just wanted to thank you for being here for Melissa these last few days," Mrs.

Fox said. She crossed her slim arms over her chest. "You have no idea how much it means to her."

Will swallowed hard. "Mrs. Fox, I—"

She held up a hand to silence him. "Now, I know you two broke up before all this happened, so I know it's been tough on you. It takes a special person to put all that aside."

"Thanks, Mrs. Fox," Will said, looking at the tiled floor. "But I have to tell you . . . I . . . I can't be her boyfriend anymore."

Mrs. Fox paled, but she kept her composure. "That's fine, Will. You do what you have to do." She took a deep breath. "Just . . . just be her friend. She has to go through some intensive therapy with a new psychiatrist, and she'll need someone to be there for her."

Will looked into her searching eyes and felt his stomach turn. *You should be there for her,* he thought. *You're her mother.* But she never had been there for Melissa. And she didn't know her daughter at all. If she did, she would know that for Melissa, friendship wasn't going to be an option. She was an all-or-nothing kind of girl.

"I'll do my best," Will said.

"I know you will," Mrs. Fox replied. She reached over and patted his arm. Her mouth was smiling, but her eyes were so sad.

Will stepped awkwardly out from under Mrs. Fox's hand and climbed the stairs. Mrs. Fox watched from the landing. He could feel her gaze still on him as he rapped lightly on Melissa's door. "Liss?" he called out. "It's me."

The door swung open, and Melissa stood beaming up at him. "There you are!" she exclaimed. She grabbed his arm, pulled him inside, and shut the door behind her. Then she jumped up and threw herself around him, arms encircling his shoulders, legs around his waist, hair underneath his nose.

"Hey," Will said, startled. "What's all this?"

"I'm just so glad to see you," she murmured, hopping back down and holding Will around his waist. "It's been so long since you've held me." She leaned back her head and gazed at him lovingly.

Will was at a loss for words, so he placed his arms around Melissa and rubbed her back mechanically.

"Shouldn't you be lying down or something?" he asked, pulling back.

Melissa's eyebrow lifted seductively. "Okay. I can lie down if you want me to." She grabbed both of his hands and walked backward toward her bed, pulling him with her.

Will's thoughts jammed up chaotically. How could she be so flirtatious? Wasn't this the same girl who only days before was having several grams of depressants pumped from her system? Did she really think that whole experience would just fade away, like some sort of bad dream?

"I'm serious, Liss," he said, freeing his hands

from her grasp and setting them on her shoulders. "You should be taking it easy. You were in the hospital hooked up to tubes, like, five seconds ago."

Melissa rolled her eyes. "I'm fine, Will. The doctors wouldn't have let me go home if I wasn't." She plopped down on the bed. "Their only condition was that I go see some counselor a couple of times a week."

"A counselor?" Will asked, sitting down beside her. Hadn't her mother just said intensive therapy?

"Yeah, I told you about this. It's just a formality. After all"—she locked eyes with Will and smiled sweetly—"I already have the best medicine. *You're* all I need to get through this. You're all I ever need." She leaned her head against his shoulder.

Will immediately tensed at her touch. He hadn't meant to, but suddenly all the guilt and anger he'd been holding down the past few days welled to the surface. His mask was off.

Melissa sensed him stiffen and pulled back, eyeing him suspiciously. "What? What is it, Will?" she asked.

He stood abruptly and walked across the room. He didn't want to see her face. He didn't want anything to interfere with what he had to do.

"There's something I need to tell you, Liss," he said to the wall. "Something important."

"I'm glad you called, Ken. I was going crazy at home." Maria slowly stirred the upper layer of whipped cream into her mochaccino and settled back against the velvet booth.

"Hey, I know the feeling," Ken replied with a rueful smile. "You know, that's the only thing I miss about football. I don't have practice to take a big chunk out of my afternoon anymore. Instead I get to sit around and go nuts thinking about stuff."

"Exactly," Maria said, nodding. "Before you called, I'd finished all my homework, cleaned my room so well you could probably lick the floor, and couldn't find anything good on TV. It almost made me wish tonight was a work night."

She took a long sip of her drink and stared out the front window of House of Java, scrutinizing the passersby. As relieved as she was to get out of her bedroom for a while, it still made her somewhat nervous being out in public. She couldn't shake the fear that Conner and Elizabeth might walk through the door at any moment.

"So how did things go with Elizabeth?" Ken asked, leaning across the table.

Maria sighed and placed her coffee cup back on the saucer. "They went nowhere," she mumbled. "I . . . um . . . I told her I didn't want to discuss it."

"What?" Ken asked, concern in his big blue eyes. "But when she came up to you at the lockers the other day, I thought you two were going to talk it out. What happened?"

"I don't know." Maria looked down guiltily. "Just changed my mind, I guess."

He frowned at her. "But why?"

She shrugged slightly. "Just because." Maria winced at her own words. She knew she came off sounding like a preschooler, but she couldn't help it. She couldn't explain her actions even to herself.

Ken squinted and shook his head. "I don't understand, Maria. I thought you said you were going to hear her out if she wanted to talk."

"Yeah, I know." Maria nervously traced the rim of the coffee cup with her fingertip. "I can't help it, Ken. Whenever she comes near me, I just freeze up. I always feel like I'm going to be sick or something."

"Did you listen to anything she had to say?" Ken asked.

"Not really. But it's not like she's about to give up." Maria took a deep breath and began telling him about all the ways Elizabeth tried to approach her during the week and how she'd blown her off each time. As she listened to herself describe everything aloud and in detail, Maria realized how immature her behavior sounded. A feeling of shame tugged at her. By the time she finished, she didn't want to look into Ken's eyes, afraid of the disappointment she'd see in them.

"I totally understand how you feel," Ken said calmly, evenly.

Maria stared at him, surprised. "You do?"

"I've been there. I know it seems much easier to just avoid things."

"Yeah," she whispered. Hearing Ken voice her exact thoughts made her feel . . . less alone.

"But," he went on, sitting up and looking right at her, "you really should let her explain, Maria. Give her a chance."

She exhaled heavily. "Why?"

"Just because," he said with a smirk.

Maria scowled at him.

"Because she's your best friend. You have to hang on to friendships like that for as long as you can." He paused and turned to gaze out the window. "I should know," he added softly.

Ken's deeply sad expression made Maria want to reach out and touch him, but she held back. She knew he was thinking about Olivia, and it made her heart turn. Compared to what Ken suffered through, Maria had it easy.

"You're right," she said, gazing down at the table. "I should listen to Elizabeth. . . . I'll give her another chance."

Ken snapped back to the present and looked at her. "Good. It'll be worth it. Trust me on this."

She met his open, earnest gaze and smiled back. "You know something, I do trust you, Ken. In fact, you're probably the only person in the world I trust right now."

*   *   *

151

Elizabeth pulled Conner's car into the driveway and looked at Megan. "You okay?" she asked.

"Yeah," Megan replied softly, staring at the glove compartment.

From the back Mrs. Sandborn muttered something unintelligible and rolled over facedown on the vinyl seat.

"Let's see if we can get her inside," Elizabeth suggested.

"Yeah," Megan mumbled again.

They hopped out of the car and opened both of the back doors. Mrs. Sandborn lay across the seat like an accident victim, arms akimbo, legs splayed awkwardly. Elizabeth, who was at the side near her feet, reached in and grabbed one arm, trying to pull Mrs. Sandborn upright. She only managed to lift her shoulder off the seat a few inches before Mrs. Sandborn let out a muffled groan and wrenched her arm free.

Again Elizabeth tried yanking on one arm while Megan pushed from the opposite side. They succeeded in raising Mrs. Sandborn to a sitting position before she wavered and jerked and crashed down again, this time with her head near Elizabeth.

Elizabeth sighed in exasperation. Her lower back was beginning to hurt, and Megan looked as if she could shatter into a billion pieces at the slightest touch.

"Mrs. Sandborn?" Elizabeth whispered, kneeling

down to shake the woman's shoulder. "Mrs. Sandborn, wake up."

Suddenly she heard the loud bang of the front door slamming, and Conner was running across the yard.

"What's going on?" he demanded. "What happened?" Elizabeth had never seen him look so angry. His eyes were wild, and his features intersected one another, as if his face were straining to leap from his skull.

"We . . . um . . . ," Elizabeth began awkwardly, "we went to the country club and found your mom sort of . . . sort of . . ."

"Wasted!" Megan shouted from the other side of the car. Her lips quivered as she stared at her brother helplessly.

"Megan! I told you a million times not to surprise Mom! Didn't I?" Conner hollered, attracting the attention of an elderly couple walking across the street.

"But I—," Megan began.

"I lent you the car as a favor," Conner ranted. "Did you have to go poking your nose into Mom's private business? How could you be so stupid?"

Megan trembled visibly, her chest heaving with deep, quick breaths. She opened her mouth to speak, but all that escaped was a rising sob. Then she turned and ran, bawling, into the house.

"And you!" Conner continued, glaring at Elizabeth.

"You had no right to interfere! This has nothing to do with you!"

Elizabeth was stunned. Conner hadn't spoken this many words to her in days, and now he stood raging at her. But all Elizabeth could focus on were his eyes. They held more pain than anger. Conner was hurting.

She touched his arm. "Conner, I was only—"

"Save it!" he hissed, ripping his arm away. "I don't want your explanations. I don't want anything from you!" He reached into the car and carefully dragged Mrs. Sandborn out, lifting her into his arms. Then slowly and steadily he carried her into the house as if he were holding a sleeping child.

melissa Fox

I was at a Catholic hospital. not that there's anything wrong with that, mind you, but it did kind of freak me out when I was zoning in front of the TV one day and a priest appeared in my doorway.

He was dressed all in black, with the telltale collar on. He was older, with graying hair, and his face was very kind looking. I must have jumped a little when I saw him there because he smiled a sort of don't-be-afraid type of smile that immediately put me at ease.

"may I come in?" he asked.

I told him sure, even though I really didn't want to talk to him. I mean, how do you say, "no. Go away!" to a priest?

He said his name was Father O'Brien and asked me how I was feeling. I told him I was all right, just a little bored. Then he got this concerned expression and asked if he could sit and talk with me awhile. Again I really didn't know how to explain that I'd rather watch Rosie, so I said that would be okay.

Father O'Brien remarked that it must get sort of lonely sometimes. He said for me to remember that I'm never totally alone, that God is always with me. All I needed to do, he said, was have faith. Then he gave a little pep talk about how belief in God is the greatest of comforts and can give us strength through the bad times.

I was still sort of dopey on the drugs, so I just nodded in the right places. At times he paused as if waiting for me to open up about myself, but I never did. And I was so glad he didn't come right out and ask me about my problems or why I was there.

Eventually he got up and left, and I never saw him again. But his words stuck with me, especially the part about where my faith lies and believing that I will be saved.

It made me think of Will. He saved me the first time this happened. He was the one who told me he loved me and made my life worth living. If it wasn't for Will, I probably wouldn't be a functioning human being. I wouldn't even be alive right now. Really. I'm not kidding.

That's why I felt so helpless when he pushed me away. That's why I felt lonely and desperate enough to swallow the pills. I was afraid I'd lost my only source of strength and comfort.

But everything is better now. I know he won't ever abandon me again. Because what we have is more than the typical girlfriend-boyfriend relationship. We have a spiritual bond. And it's forever.

My faith is with Will. I've never needed anything else but him. And I never will.

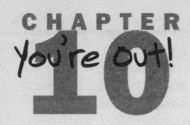
Once again the Sandborn house was enveloped in silence, except for the sickening sounds coming from Mrs. Sandborn's bathroom. Megan was locked in her room, refusing to respond to Elizabeth's knocks, and Conner was in with his mom, helping her with her prayer to the porcelain god. Eventually Elizabeth couldn't listen anymore and crept down to the living room.

She restlessly circled the long, floral-print sofa until the sun setting outside cast the room in shadows. *He hates me,* Elizabeth thought, her heart pounding as she recalled Conner's tirade. *He hates me because I found out about his secret.*

Elizabeth heard a door open and click shut upstairs. She froze, her heart in her throat, as she listened to the sound of Conner's heavy footsteps descending the stairs. He walked into the living room, his face drained of all energy and emotion.

"Conner," Elizabeth said, crossing her arms over her stomach and gripping her elbows.

He jumped slightly at the sound of her voice, and

a scowl worked its way into his features. "What are you doing here?"

There was anguish behind his angry stare. It made her want to go hold him and comfort him. But she held back. She knew Conner would lash out at her if she got too close.

"I—I was just worried," she replied. "How's your mother?"

He took a few steps into the room, glaring at Elizabeth. "This is none of your business."

Elizabeth took a deep breath. "I just want to help."

"We do not *need* your help," he said through clenched teeth.

The hostility in his voice made her wince. "But—"

"No!" Conner balled his hand into a fist and slammed it against the wall. "Haven't you done enough already?"

Elizabeth jumped. For the second time that day she'd seen someone completely transformed before her eyes. First Mrs. Sandborn, and now Conner.

He bowed his head, took a deep, audible breath through his nose, and then looked Elizabeth directly in the eye.

"I want you out," he said, his green eyes sharp with anger.

Elizabeth's heart seemed to freeze as she searched his face for a glimmer of doubt. She found none. "You—you don't mean that," she whispered, tears stinging her eyes as she stepped toward him.

"I just said it," he muttered, pushing past her. He stood in front of the darkened window and turned his back to Elizabeth.

Elizabeth could feel her knees buckling and quickly reached out for the couch to steady herself. How could he do this to her? Didn't he realize that by focusing on her, he was just avoiding the real issue? He was so stubborn and so blind. He was just going to spend his entire life pushing everyone away, even if all they wanted was to be there for him.

Staring at Conner's rigid form, Elizabeth suddenly felt something new stir deep inside her chest.

Anger.

She pulled herself up straight, lifted her chin, and walked up right behind him. The tears still wanted to come, but she forced them to hold back.

"Fine, I'll go," Elizabeth spat. She allowed herself a wry smile when she saw him wince slightly at her tone. "But your mom needs serious help, Conner. She has a problem."

Conner whirled around, his expression venomous. His face was just inches from hers, and part of Elizabeth still wanted to hold him and tell him everything was going to be fine. But they were past that. Way past it. "No one wants your advice," he said evenly. "And no one wants you here."

Elizabeth's stomach twisted as she tried desperately to hold his gaze without breaking down. A thin blue vein throbbed in the middle of Conner's forehead as he leaned in even closer. Elizabeth held her breath. Then Conner spoke, and his words were like a gunshot to her heart.

"*I* don't want you here."

"What *is* it, Will?" Melissa asked again, her voice rising to a shout.

Will blew his breath out slowly, letting himself feel all the emotions he'd been suppressing the past few days. Then he turned and met Melissa's unsteady gaze.

"It's over, Liss," he said simply, quietly. "I know you think we're back together again and that everything's fine, but it's not. I just can't be with you anymore. You have to accept that."

He waited for her to respond, but her expression remained intact. She didn't even blink.

Will figured she was waiting for an explanation. He walked over to the bed and stooped down beside her, grabbing up her hand awkwardly. "It's not that I don't care about you, because I do," he said emphatically. "I just can't take the way things have become. The lying, the guilt trips, the ganging up on . . . people. It's not what I want."

Again he paused for a reply, but Melissa still sat frozen in place, giving no clues to her underlying mood. *This is easier than I thought it would be,* Will remarked to himself. *Too easy.*

"Anyhow, I think it's better for us—for you—if we were apart. I can't be your crutch anymore, Liss. You need to learn how to live without me." He reached up and gently cupped her chin between his thumb and index finger. "Do you get what I'm saying?"

Melissa finally stirred—more internally than externally. He watched as a darkness crept in behind her eyes, and her chin trembled ever so slightly in his grasp.

Here it comes, he thought, bracing himself for her violent sobbing, her urgent pleas for him to stay.

But she did none of those things. Suddenly, without any warning, Melissa's fist flew up in front of his face, her knuckles colliding with his left eye. A blinding light seared through his head, and he fell backward against the carpeting.

"You lying, cheating bastard!" she screamed.

As Will's vision slowly restored itself, he could see Melissa looming over him, shouting curse words and pelting him with nearby objects. Paperback books and stuffed animals bounced off his head, and a bottle of perfume hit him in the ribs.

"You can't do this to me!" she yelled. "You can't!"

He scrambled to his feet and backed toward the door, shielding his face with his arms.

"If you cared about me, you wouldn't do this!" she continued, flinging a tennis shoe at him.

"I do care, Liss," he said, ducking.

"Why don't you just plunge a knife into me? Why not just kill me and get it over with?" Her face was frantic and wild.

Will felt like a snake. The angry terror in her voice scared him, and for a split second he considered backing down. But he knew he couldn't. It was done. There was nothing to revive.

Melissa ran out of nearby projectiles and ceased her attack, her eyes darting feverishly around the room for another worthy missile. Will took the opportunity to bolt for the door and open it.

He looked back at Melissa, who was reaching for an object on her nightstand. "You really should give counseling a try, Liss," he said earnestly. "Learn to help yourself."

Will heard a furious grunt, and then his own face came flying toward him, encased in a heavy brass frame. He quickly slipped out the door and shut it just as a loud crash sounded on the other side.

Will rushed down the stairs and almost knocked over Mrs. Fox, who was on her way up.

"Will?" she said with a gasp. "What's going on up there?"

"I'm sorry, Mrs. Fox," Will said, his face burning. Then he turned and pushed through the front door. More than anything in the world he needed to get away from that room, away from that house. Away from Melissa.

As he stepped out of the house into the warm,

evening air, Will felt a strange lifting sensation come over him—something he hadn't felt in years.

He felt free.

"Where am I going?" Elizabeth mumbled aloud.

After her heart-wrenching argument with Conner, Elizabeth had thrown a few things in her backpack and stormed from the house. For several minutes she had wandered along the empty street, sobbing and thinking about Conner. But eventually the burst of emotion that propelled her down the road subsided, and it occurred to her that she had no place to go. Her own home had been destroyed in the earthquake, Lila had practically driven her from her house, Maria wasn't speaking to her, and now Conner had tossed her out of his life. She was alone. A transient with a vinyl backpack.

Elizabeth plopped down on the curb in front of a big, white-stucco house. Her back ached from trying to lift Mrs. Sandborn, and the sides of her shoes were cutting deep grooves in her feet.

"Why didn't you grab your tennis shoes?" she said. "Who the heck runs away in clogs?" Of course, she hadn't actually run away. And it wasn't as if Conner had given her time to think straight. Just the thought of his irate expression seemed to put another crack in her heart.

Elizabeth's anger had melted away and left behind nothing but hurt. It hurt her to see Conner suffering under so much strain, and it hurt her to know that he didn't want her help.

A loud honk startled Elizabeth from her thoughts. She looked up to find Jessica pulling the Jeep alongside the curb.

"Hey, you," said Jessica, lowering the window. "Hop in."

"How . . . how did you know?" Elizabeth asked as she climbed into the passenger side of the car.

Jessica smiled sympathetically. "Megan called. She said you and Conner had a bad fight and that you . . . had to leave. I've been driving around for five minutes trying to find you. You okay?"

The compassion in her sister's voice made Elizabeth break down all over again. She crumpled against the seat as wave after wave of intense sobs passed through her body.

Jessica leaned over and put both arms around Elizabeth, steadying her. "Shhh. It's all right," she whispered. "I'm taking you home."

Home, Elizabeth thought. She wished that she was actually going back to her house. To her comfortable room, where everything was familiar and safe. Knowing she would be returning to the Fowlers' wasn't much of a comfort. But as Elizabeth leaned against Jessica's shoulder, letting her tears spill out onto her cardigan, a sense of calm gradually came over her.

At least she'd be back with Jessica. Back with her

mom and dad, who had practically become strangers.

"You want to talk about it?" Jessica said once Elizabeth's crying had subsided.

Elizabeth shook her head. "Not now," she replied weakly. "I just need a little while to, you know, process it all."

"I understand." Jessica sat back in her seat and gestured at the house in front of them. "These people probably think we've got them under surveillance. You okay to go?"

Elizabeth nodded wearily.

As they drove off, Elizabeth put a hand on her sister's arm. "Thanks," she said hoarsely.

"Hey, no biggie," Jessica replied, grinning. "I'm sure I owe you one anyway."

Elizabeth looked out the window and watched the rows of darkened houses pass by. She felt better. Being with her sister was a huge comfort. But what about Conner and Megan? Elizabeth knew she was never going to forget the pain and confusion she had seen on Megan's face. Or the anger and loathing she saw on Conner's.

What was going to happen to them?

Lila Fowler
on Sisters

I've never had a sister, and I'm glad. I couldn't handle some nosy brat digging through my stuff, arguing over who gets dibs on the Porsche, wanting advice on this and that. It's been bad enough having Jessica and Elizabeth take over my domain—I couldn't imagine dealing with it 24/7 for my entire life.

But sometimes, during occasional lapses in rational thought, I wonder if having a sib might offer some perks.

Elizabeth is back here tonight. I guess the poor family that took her in finally had enough. There I was, sitting in my room studying, when I was interrupted by the twins gabbing away in the next room. (Okay, so I was doing my toenails and jamming out to the stereo, but still! A girl's gotta have some downtime, right?) I could hear Liz's high-pitched sobs and Jess's hushed tones. Obviously something major was going on. I turned down the music and tried to hear what it was about, but nothing distinct came through. Eventually they lapsed into that sisterly chatter of theirs—those muffled chirps that can cut through walls like a hydraulic drill. Now Lizzie seems <u>all</u> better. Must not be too terrible to have a second version of yourself to open up to now and then.

So I got to thinking, maybe I've missed out. Maybe it would actually be cool to have a sister. Just as long as she isn't the type that would steal my boyfriends and hog all the hot water.

Jeremy couldn't believe his good luck. It was Friday evening and here he was, sitting in a cozy dining room with Jessica. So far, so good. His mother hadn't been called in to work, his dad was feeling much better, his car had started, and the restaurant was exactly what he'd expected—cheap but good. Did this mean he could finally relax and completely enjoy himself?

"So then the principal comes over the intercom and says, 'We've been having problems with our com system, but we think the matter has been fixed. If you can't hear this announcement in your class-room, please send a student to the office immedi-ately.'" Jessica laughed and shook her head, her glossy blond waves caressing her bare shoulders.

"That's nothing," Jeremy said, chuckling. "We once had this big assembly on fire safety and ended up trapped in the auditorium because the main doors got stuck. The fire marshall was right there to make out the code violation."

"Ah, school," Jessica commented. "It's hard to be-lieve we have less than a year to go before freedom."

169

"As long as we survive the year, that is," Jeremy said, thinking of his father and how everything was being held together by a very thin thread. Immediately he regretted it. Why'd he have to douse the good mood with a negative remark like that? "So . . . ," he began, rapidly switching gears. "How's your scampi?"

Jessica lowered her lids halfway and murmured, "Mmmm," a gesture Jeremy found incredibly alluring. "It's fantastic," she exclaimed. "How's your lasagna?"

"Great. Although I'm pretty easy to please," Jeremy admitted. "I think all Italian food in general is evidence of God."

Jessica nodded. "I agree. Here, try this." She stabbed a shrimp with her fork and twirled it in a few strands of noodles. Then she raised her arm and carefully guided the morsel into Jeremy's mouth. "What do you think?" she asked.

Jeremy gave a slight hum of approval, but he was only vaguely aware of the garlicky sensation on his tongue. Instead he was focused on the way the glow from the candle sconce lit up Jessica's hair as she leaned across the table, giving the effect of a halo.

"Oops. There's a little spot of butter on your cheek," Jessica said softly. She lifted her hand and gently rubbed the side of his mouth with her fingers.

Jeremy smiled. The evening was going beyond his expectations. Everything felt so *right*.

"I think I got it," Jessica said, sitting back in her chair. Then she tilted her head and studied his face.

Jeremy hoped his expression didn't reveal the swooning sensation he felt.

A waiter in a white shirt and shiny black vest suddenly materialized next to them and began clearing their dishes off the table. "May I get you anything else?" he asked. "Some coffee, perhaps? Or dessert?"

Jeremy glanced over at Jessica.

"No, thanks," she replied, waving her hand. "I've already reached maximum density. You go ahead."

"Uh . . . no, thanks," Jeremy said to the waiter. "I guess just the check, please."

The man gave a single nod and walked off. Jeremy hoped he never returned. He hadn't really thought far enough ahead to consider what they would do after dinner. After their recent run of bad luck, he figured it would be a miracle if they even made it through the meal without some sort of natural disaster befalling them. Now that things had gone so smoothly, he was afraid trying something new was pushing his good fortune to the limits.

Jessica stared out a nearby window. "That boardwalk is relatively new, isn't it?"

He squinted through the glass at the shop-lined walkway. "I think so."

"Hey, I have an idea." Jessica faced him again, her eyes sparkling. "Do you want to go for a walk over there? It's such a nice night, and I should definitely work off some of these carbs I loaded up on. Can we save whatever you had planned for another date?"

Another date? Jeremy's heart ballooned.

"No problem," he said. "We can save it for"—he paused, relishing the words—"the next time."

Darkness slowly seeped into the sky like spilled ink. The breeze skimming off the ocean was soft and cool. Jessica listened to the rumble of the nearby surf and the rhythm of their shoes against the boardwalk's wooden planks. *I feel like I'm on another planet,* she thought happily. *Someplace where stress doesn't even exist.*

Normally she'd be chatting up a storm, trying to fill the empty spaces with lighthearted patter. But with Jeremy she didn't feel the need. The silence between them as they strolled along the wooden deck was cozy and peaceful instead of awkward.

Eventually they wandered over to the deck railing and stood gazing out at the ocean. After watching the ripples of waves glisten under the evening stars for a few minutes, Jessica turned and stared at Jeremy. She studied his profile—strong yet boyish, chiseled yet gentle. She loved how the side of his face sloped into a shallow hollow beneath his cheekbone, making him look slightly aristocratic and very, very kissable.

Jeremy glanced upward at the sky, a slight smile creasing his cheek.

"What're you thinking about?" she whispered.

"It's stupid," he said.

"No, tell me," she urged, playfully pushing her hand against his chest.

"It's nothing really," he mumbled down at his loafers. "I was just remembering watching the stars when I was a little kid. I didn't know exactly what they were, and I assumed it was heaven shining through tiny holes in a big, black tapestry."

"That's so sweet," she teased, reaching out to touch him again.

Jeremy lifted his head and stared at her, all seriousness. "I feel like I'm there right now. In heaven."

Jessica's heart jumped as she locked eyes with him. "Wow. How many times did you practice *that* line?"

Jeremy grinned. "About a hundred and twenty-five," he said with a shrug. Then he lifted his hand and softly cupped her face, drawing her toward him. "But it's still true."

And then they were kissing. Jessica closed her eyes and enjoyed the sweet, tingling connection between them. It was nice, warm, and . . . right. Like the waves always seemed to know which direction to flow, her lips and Jeremy's seemed to find each other just as naturally.

For the first time in months things were how they should be. And Jessica felt happy.

Will was on a mission. He knew what he needed to do: It was time to make things right with Jessica.

Now that he'd untangled himself from Melissa, he no longer needed to feel torn or guilty about every move he made. He could follow his gut. And his gut was steering him all the way to Jessica's house.

As he drove his Chevy Blazer toward the Fowler mansion, his chest tightened with excitement and impatience. He should have done this a long time ago. Before everything went so haywire. It was his fault Jessica had suffered so much—his fault that Melissa went so far. An apology was probably too little, too late, but it was all he had to offer. If he didn't come clean with her, he'd never forgive himself. The trick was going to be getting Jessica to listen to him. Up until now she'd always pushed him away.

This time he wouldn't let her.

Will made the final turn and pulled up along the curb near the house. He couldn't park right in front because another car was slowly coming out of the driveway, blocking his path. Will caught a glimpse of a guy's shadow at the wheel as the Mercedes backed onto the street and drove off. Then he looked up and saw Jessica standing on the porch, waving.

Will's heart sank. It was obvious by the glow on Jessica's smiling face that she'd just been on a date— and a fantastic one at that. The realization drained his determination.

What'd you expect, Simmons? he scolded himself. *Did you think she'd mope around forever? You blew your chance. Blew it big time.*

He sighed heavily. Like it or not, Jessica was moving on. And after everything he put her through, she certainly deserved to feel happy. Maybe he should just take off and go back home. Why ruin her moment?

A sadness filled him as he watched her. She was truly stunning.

For some reason, Jessica remained on the front stoop long after the Mercedes had disappeared. She leaned against the wall and stared up at the stars, smiling mysteriously. *Why is she still outside?* he wondered.

Will decided to take it as a sign. He came all this way to talk to her, and there she was, right before his eyes. It was now or never.

Quickly he hopped out of his car and jogged across the lawn toward the porch. At the same moment Jessica turned to head into the house.

"Jessica!" he shouted, accelerating his pace. "Jess, wait!"

She whirled around, her eyes wide with surprise. "Will?"

It killed him to see the joy instantly disappear from her face.

"What are you doing here?" she asked, stiffening.

"Please, hear me out, Jess," he said urgently. "There's something I have to tell you." He caught his breath and stepped into the porch light, meeting her gaze head-on. "Do you think it's possible . . . I mean, could you maybe . . . give me a chance to apologize to you?"

Jessica stared at him for a long moment, the color draining out of her skin. Finally she said in a voice barely above a whisper, "It's possible."

Will exhaled in relief. "Jess, I'm . . . I'm so sorry.

175

About everything. I just don't know where to begin." He lifted his hands in a helpless gesture and looked away, a fierce shame surfacing from within. "I didn't want to hurt you, Jess. I made a horrible mistake and tried to undo it all with lies. You didn't deserve anything that happened."

"I'm glad someone finally figured that out," Jessica said.

Will sighed. "What I'm trying to say is, it's over," he continued. "Things will be better from now on. I promise you that. I just hope that maybe, you could someday consider me . . . a friend?" He swallowed hard and forced himself to look into her eyes.

Jessica stood there quietly, scrutinizing his face. Then slowly, surely, her body seemed to relax, and the glow rekindled inside her.

Finally she shrugged slightly and half-smiled. "It's not impossible."

JEREMY AAMES

12:15 A.M.

Jessica. Jessica. Jessica. Jessica.
Jessica . . .

JESSICA WAKEFIELD
12:16 A.M.

Jeremy. Jeremy. Jeremy. Will. No! I mean, Jeremy. Jeremy. _Jer-e-my_.

I knew this would happen.

What right does Elizabeth have to try and tell us how to handle things? We never said we wanted her to be a part of our family. Just because we give her a room for a few weeks, she thinks she's allowed full disclosure of our lives?

But what's she going to do now that she knows everything?

Maybe she'll follow me around preaching warm, fuzzy psychobabble and telling me how a good cry can work wonders.

Maybe, though, she'll actually stay away and let my life go back to the way it was. The way it was before Elizabeth.

Check out the **all-new....**

..... (Sweet Valley Web site—)

www.sweetvalley.com

New Features

Cool Prizes

The **ONLY** *official* Web site!

Hot Links

(And much more!)

BFYR 202